"Hold Out Your Hands,"
She Said Crisply

Dawn moved away from her loom, picked up a bundle of yarn and turned to Logan.

"Are you going to tie me up?" he asked.

"Don't tempt me," she muttered.

"Does the thought of tying me up tempt you?" he inquired meaningfully.

She looked up with wide green eyes, unable to conceal her shock.

"Didn't you know?" he asked. "Some people like it that way."

"Tied up?" she responded in disbelief.

"Mmm."

"Do you?" she asked, only to flush as she heard her own words. The thought of Logan playing sensual games both fascinated and frightened her.

"Never tried it. Never wanted to. But if that's what it takes to turn you on—" a corner of his mouth tilted up "—I aim to please."

D1052297

Dear Reader,

Welcome to Silhouette! Our goal is to give you hours of unbeatable reading pleasure, and we hope you'll enjoy each month's six new Silhouette Desires. These sensual, provocative love stories are both believable and compelling—sometimes they're poignant, sometimes humorous, but always enjoyable.

Indulge yourself. Experience all the passion and excitement of falling in love along with our heroine as she meets the irresistible man of her dreams and together they overcome all obstacles in the path to a happy ending.

If this is your first Desire, I hope it'll be the first of many. If you're already a Silhouette Desire reader, thanks for your support! Look for some of your favorite authors in the coming months: Stephanie James, Diana Palmer, Dixie Browning, Ann Major and Doreen Owens Malek, to name just a few.

Happy reading!

Isabel Swift
Senior Editor

SDRL-7/85

ELIZABETH LOWELL
The Fire of Spring

Silhouette Desire

Published by Silhouette Books New York

America's Publisher of Contemporary Romance

SILHOUETTE BOOKS
300 E. 42nd St., New York, N.Y. 10017

Copyright © 1986 by Ann Maxwell

All rights reserved, including the right to reproduce
this book or portions thereof in any form whatsoever.
For information address Silhouette Books,
300 E. 42nd St., New York, N.Y. 10017

ISBN: 0-373-05265-0

First Silhouette Books printing March 1986

All the characters in this book are fictitious. Any
resemblance to actual persons, living or dead, is purely
coincidental.

SILHOUETTE, SILHOUETTE DESIRE and colophon are
registered trademarks of the publisher.

America's Publisher of Contemporary Romance

Printed in the U.S.A.

Books by Elizabeth Lowell

Silhouette Desire

Summer Thunder #77
The Fire of Spring #265

Silhouette Intimate Moments

The Danvers Touch #18
Lover in the Rough #34
Summer Games #57
Forget Me Not #72
A Woman without Lies #81
Traveling Man #97
Valley of the Sun #109
Sequel #128

ELIZABETH LOWELL

writes in several fields. When friends ask her why she decided to write "*romances*, of all things," she just smiles. She has been married for eighteen years to the only man she has ever loved. How can she help but write novels that celebrate love and life?

To my editor
Pat Smith
lost and found

Come, fill the Cup, and in the fire of Spring
Your winter garment of Repentance fling.

From the Rubáiyát of Omar Khayyám
Translated by Edward FitzGerald

One

Spring was a distant promise slowly creeping up the base of the high peaks surrounding Aspen, Colorado. It wasn't a promise that was being greeted with great delight in the town. Spring was the awkward season—too warm for ski tourists and too cold for any other kind. Spring was gloppy snow, patchy ski runs and sparsely populated boutiques. It was also the time when year-round residents breathed a collective sigh and mentally prepared for the next onslaught of tourists shedding dollars the way a cat sheds hair.

From where Dawn Sheridan looked out the window of her tiny cabin, she could see only occasional glimpses of Aspen flung across the base of towering mountains. She was miles out of town. Her view consisted of snow, bare-branched aspens, shaggy evergreens and winter-wrapped peaks. The development she lived in had been slapped together during one of the frantic tourist booms of previous years. Despite its name, Aspen Acres was just too faraway from the trendy attractions of the real Aspen to attract renters.

Because Dawn's downhill skiing abilities were as limited as her budget, and her bed and barhopping abilities were nonexistent, she didn't mind being removed from Aspen's glittering action. For her the isolated cabin was perfect. It allowed her to live close to her major markets and still spend quiet hours designing and executing the weavings that lived so vividly in her mind.

With green eyes that saw patterns where other people saw simply random colors and lines, Dawn measured the magnificent country outside her window. Beyond Aspen, down at the lower elevations, spring would be arriving in a few weeks, pushing the snow into the cover of the forest, making creeks burst with meltwater and bringing a fragile blush of green to the grazing lands. In a month the first calves would be born into a raw April wind, and their mothers would hover protectively, using their much larger bodies to shelter the tiny russet babies.

Dawn had always loved spring, seeing in the tender, fierce persistence of the season a pattern that gave her hope for her own life. Each year spring won out over winter ice. Each year calves were born and grew and ultimately had their own young, feeding on the rich grass pushing up from the earth that only shortly before had been held in winter's rigid grasp. The pattern of renewal was a promise as enduring as Colorado's granite mountains.

Dawn hoped that someday, perhaps, the promise would be kept for her as well.

Unbidden, the image of golden-brown eyes condensed in Dawn's memory, eyes that could be as clear as amber and as unforgiving as stone—or as warm as cognac reflecting an evening fire. His hair could be like fire, too. A dark, burnished bronze with molten gold threaded in its depths. Thick, with a sensual richness like coarse silk sliding between her fingers. And his mouth—so controlled, so hot, melting her the way spring melts winter ice.

Dawn stared out the window, but it was the past her eyes focused on. Usually she tried not to think about Logan Garrett. She rarely succeeded. Three years wasn't nearly long enough to forget the strength of his arms around her, the almost shocking hardness of his body pressed against hers, and the truly shocking response of her own body. She had felt nothing like that before or since Logan Garrett. She hadn't known that lightning was a natural part of her flesh, that there was a hunger and a passion in her that could make her tremble like an aspen in a summer storm, that she had been born to come apart in one man's hands.

Yet Logan hadn't even made love to her. Not really. Not completely. He had simply teased her expertly, neither knowing nor caring that she was totally inexperienced, unable either to control her responses or to understand them. She had thought it was love that had freed the passion within her. Her love for him. His love for her.

Her full mouth turned down in a sad, taut curve. *Love. Ah, Dawn, what a child you were at eighteen. You had told yourself all your life that you weren't like your mother. You would never be any man's woman just for the asking. Then along came Logan. He didn't even have to ask. All he had to do was look at you and you trembled. Silly little aspen leaf. So green. You believed only in summer's heat. Then the frost came.*

Yet Dawn couldn't help wondering what it would have been like if Logan hadn't turned away in disgust when she had simply looked at him, her eyes full of helpless tears, hearing his words slice through her eager flesh to the bone.

Dawn, I know how much you want this ranch. You don't have to leave the Lazy W just because I own it now. You can stay as long as you're my mistress. But I'm warning you—

the first time you even look at another man I'll strip you naked and leave you in the town square.

But I love you, Logan!

Mary Sue's daughter loving a man? What kind of a fool do you think I am? For your information, my name is Logan Garrett, not Joe Garrett. My brother couldn't tell the difference between a woman and a money-hungry slut like Mary Sue. I can. You're here because you want the ranch, not me. You want to tie me in knots until I give you the Lazy W on a solid-gold platter. It won't work, baby. Your mama dumped Joe and married your daddy because she wanted to be mistress of the Lazy W. Now the ranch is mine. She'll never set foot on it again, hear me?

Then Dawn had cried and Logan had turned his back, telling her that he would expect her answer in the morning.

In the morning Dawn had been gone. Life hadn't been easy for Mary Sue's daughter. Dawn had learned very young to recognize the patterns in people as well as in cloth. The previous night had taught her that she couldn't trust herself when Logan touched her. She knew that if she stayed within his reach she would become what he already believed her to be—a tramp. He would destroy her as surely as her mother had destroyed his brother.

Logan wanted revenge for his dead brother, not love.

Dawn knew that, yet she still felt heat uncurl deep within her at just the memory of Logan's eyes watching her. She was haunted by the stubborn belief that he had wanted more from her than he asked for, that the love she had for him would one day be answered.

Stop it! Dawn said to herself harshly. Her long, tapered fingers curled into fists. *Logan Garrett wanted the temporary use of your body. Period. The rest of you didn't interest him. So you refused him. It's been three years. Forget him the way he's forgotten you.*

It should have been easy to forget the rough-voiced man who had casually assumed that she was her mother's daughter, available to any male who had an itch to be scratched. It should have been easy to forget, but it wasn't. Logan was the man who had taught Dawn that she had the same sensuality that Mary Sue Sheridan had, the same capacity for passion that had earned her mother a reputation that the daughter still hadn't lived down.

Grimly Dawn turned her mind from the pattern of her past. There was nothing new to learn from it. The warp was laid, the weft woven through, the bleak pattern clear and irrevocable. Brooding over it would change nothing except the pattern of her present, making it as bleak as her past. She had made the choice three years ago. A new pattern. Colors and possibilities where none had existed before. Not guarantees, though. Just possibilities. At twenty-one, Dawn knew the difference.

She stood on tiptoe and stretched completely, throwing graceful shadows as she swayed and twisted, loosening muscles grown taut with hours of uninterrupted weaving. Every day she promised herself that she would get up more often and stretch or take a walk around the cabin. Every day she became lost in the designs she was weaving, forgetting time, forgetting the past, forgetting everything except the near-magical creation of richly colored cloth where nothing had been before but heaped skeins of yarn.

It had been the same today. Normally she would have spent an hour skiing cross-country at dawn, knowing that if she didn't get some kind of exercise she eventually would be too restless to concentrate on weaving. Which was exactly what had happened today. She just had finished the last of the orders—napkins and place mats, belts and scarves and ponchos—that had been contracted by the Aspen boutiques that sold her weavings, but she hadn't started on any new cloth yet. She had enough money to get through spring and into summer before she had to take more orders. If she wanted to work more she could make more money, but money for its own sake had never interested Dawn.

She would rather take the time to work on tapestries that pleased only her and a few gallery owners scattered throughout the West. The patterns she created for her scenic tapestries were simple, impressionistic, richly textured and unique. She had been creating and weaving such tapestries for as long as she could remember. Her earliest memories were a montage of colorful yarns and looms of different sizes, and through it all wove the dry, calm voice of her grandmother speaking of traditions as old as man and patterns as new as sunrise.

Even today, the big four-harness loom Dawn used was modeled after her grandmother's old loom. Of all the things that had vanished the night her father lost the Sheridan's family ranch to Logan Garrett in a poker game, the loss of her grandmother's loom hurt Dawn the most. With an unconscious sigh she turned back to her own loom. Though it was less than three years old, constant use had put an unmistakable patina on the wood. The loom was empty now, having neither neatly aligned yarns to create the warp nor various yarn-filled shuttles waiting to be used in making the weft that would fill out the weaving. Dawn felt like the loom. Empty. Waiting.

A flash of bronze and black caught Dawn's eye. A huge lean cat strolled into the room. The cat's short fur was fluffed against the cold, blurring the usually distinctive tiger striping. The animal stood at her feet and yowled demandingly. Smiling, Dawn held out her arms.

"Hello, Prowl," she murmured. "Little nippy out there for your taste this morning?"

Prowl sprang up and rubbed her head under Dawn's chin. Dawn returned the caress with a catlike movement of her own, enjoying the animal's silky fur. Prowl permitted it for a moment, then flowed down out of Dawn's arms, leaving a few shiny hairs behind. She brushed them away automatically.

"You know," she said, "if you were just a little bigger and I had Grandmother's old spindle, I could collect all this fur and spin it into something useful."

Prowl stood in the entrance to the kitchen alcove. Her long tail twitched in a motion that was both question and demand.

Dawn fed the cat before taking her sketch pad in one hand and starting toward her rocking chair. No matter how slowly she rocked or how calm she forced her breathing to be, no ideas came to her. There was a restlessness in her that would brook no soothing.

Get it together, Dawn, she told herself impatiently. *It's too soon for spring fever.*

Not down in the valley it isn't, she retorted. *On the Lazy W the snow will be melting soon and—*

You're not on the Lazy W. Spring is later here, remember? And if you've forgotten that, kindly remember that you'll never see the Lazy W again except in memories.

The sound of a car laboring up the frozen driveway stopped Dawn's interior tug-of-war. She set aside her sketch pad and stood up. She wasn't expecting anyone, unless one of the boutiques had gotten desperate for a shipment and was saving her the trip into town tomorrow. She hurried to the window and pressed her forehead against the smooth, cold glass. At first she didn't recognize the woman climbing awkwardly out of her car. Then Dawn saw a flash of honey-blond hair.

"Kathy?" breathed Dawn in disbelief.

The woman turned sideways, revealing the outline of a pregnancy that was well advanced.

"Kathy!" called Dawn, flinging open the cabin's front door. "What's wrong? No! Don't move an inch until I get there. You could slip and—"

Dawn swooped down on the other woman and took a firm grip on her, making sure that the steps to the cabin were negotiated safely. When the front door was shut, she turned on her guest and demanded, "What on earth are you doing here?"

"Gee, thanks," Kathy said, laughing and unbuttoning the turquoise wool coat she was wearing. "Haven't seen me in almost three years and the first thing you ask is why I'm here. Got any herb tea around this place?"

"Tea?" asked Dawn, her shock clear. Kathy's desire for hot, strong coffee had been as great as any cowhand's. "Herb tea?"

Kathy grimaced. "Yeah, I know. Wretched stuff. But the doctor told me to take up weak tea for the duration of the pregnancy."

"Why?"

"He's got some crazy notion that caffeine makes for small babies, and since I'm carrying twins, I've got to be careful."

"Twins," said Dawn slowly. Then, smiling and shaking her head, she added, "Again?"

"Hey, if it works, why fix it, right? The first twins worked just fine after they put on a little weight."

Dawn laughed and hugged Kathy suddenly. "Oh, Kathy, it's great to see you. Letters and phone calls are nice, but—"

"Yeah," said Kathy, hugging Dawn in return. "I know what you mean."

"Sit down," said Dawn, taking the coat and leading Kathy to an overstuffed chair that had seen better days.

Prowl had beaten both women to the chair. Dawn scooped the cat up and dumped her unceremoniously into the padded rocker. Kathy settled in and propped her feet on the ratty ottoman with a weary sigh. Dawn gave her a worried look.

"Does Dale know you're here?" asked Dawn. She knew how protective Kathy's husband was. It seemed unlikely that anything short of an emergency would convince him to let Kathy drive alone over a hundred miles of mountain roads in her condition.

"Yeah, he knows. He's waiting in Aspen. He didn't like it, but he agreed it had to be done."

"Why?" asked Dawn. "What's wrong?" Then every muscle in her body tightened with an uncanny premonition. Now she knew why she had been so restless. "Logan," she breathed.

"You and that part-Indian grandmother of yours," said Kathy plaintively. "Never could fool either one of you worth a damn."

Dawn spun around and walked into the miniature kitchen. "First the tea," she said almost desperately, trying to bring her shaking hands under control before Kathy could see them. "Then you can tell me what's wrong. Are you hungry?" she asked, reaching for a container of mixed teas and nearly knocking it off the counter with her suddenly clumsy hands.

"Got anything without salt in it?" asked Kathy in a resigned voice.

"No salt, either?" asked Dawn in disbelief.

"Just for the last few weeks. Ever had a saltless egg?"

"Er, no."

"God, I envy you," said Kathy feelingly.

Dawn couldn't help smiling. She had always been drawn to Kathy's earthy directness. Kathy hadn't allowed such trivial things as her brother Logan's hatred of the Sheridans to interfere with her choice of playmates. Nearly three years older than Dawn, Kathy had befriended and defended Dawn during the years when they had both attended the same small rural schools. When Dawn had been brutally teased about her mother's "boyfriends," Kathy had stepped in and held the tormentors at bay until Dawn could escape. Dawn's natural grace and stillness made a perfect foil for Kathy's mischievous, volatile personality. In spite of their differences in age and personality, and the fact that there had been little opportunity as they grew up to play together outside of school, the girls had become enduring friends.

By the time the herb tea was brewed and fresh fruit put out, Dawn's normal coordination had returned. She managed to set the tea in front of Kathy without spilling it into her mountainously rounded lap. As Dawn turned away to get napkins, the heavy single braid of her black hair swung gently against her waist.

"That's another thing I envy you," said Kathy.

"What?"

"You don't have to worry about jammy little fingers getting in all that glorious hair. I had to cut mine."

Dawn laughed softly and handed Kathy a turquoise napkin that had bronze threads running through it at random, suggesting a sun-streaked sky.

"Beautiful," said Kathy, taking the napkin.

"Oh, I don't know," responded Dawn. "I always liked blond, myself."

"Not your hair—your napkins. Bet they sell like crazy in all those flashy Aspen boutiques."

Dawn returned with her own cup of coffee. She picked up Prowl and sat down in the same motion. The cat was barely disturbed.

"Do they?" persisted Kathy.

"Sell?"

Kathy nodded.

"Yes." Dawn's green eyes fastened intently on the woman who was both her best friend and the sister of the man who had won Dawn's inheritance in a poker game and then suggested that she make her living as his mistress. "Is it money, Kathy? Are you finally going to let me pay back the $5,000 you loaned me when I left the Lazy W?"

"Well, kind of," said Kathy, sipping at the herb tea.

Dawn smiled and shook her head slowly. "Kathy," she said, touching the other woman's arm, "there was no need for you to drive up here to ask for something I've been trying to give you for more than a year. The money is in a special account," she continued, setting aside her coffee. "I'll write a check and—"

"No," said Kathy firmly.

Dawn was startled. It was the same answer she had gotten every time she had tried to pay Kathy in the past, but it wasn't the answer Dawn had expected this time. Slowly she sank back down into the rocking chair that she used when thinking up new designs. "Then what can I do to pay you back?"

Kathy took a deep breath and said in a rush, "Come and take care of Logan for eight weeks while he gets well."

"What?" asked Dawn, stunned.

"You know. All the things you used to do when your dad and mom were in Vegas. See that the right stuff is ordered for the house and the ranch and that the hands are fed and that Logan doesn't get out of bed for at least two weeks and—"

"Kathy," interrupted Dawn desperately, "*what's wrong*?"

"If eight weeks is too long then make it six or even four," Kathy rushed on, her light brown eyes pleading with Dawn to understand. "Oh please, Dawn. He's killing himself just like Joe did."

"Alcohol?" asked Dawn in utter disbelief, remembering how very wary Logan was of the drug that had killed his brother. "Logan is drinking too much?"

"No way. Not after Joe. It's just—" Kathy hesitated.

"Gambling?" asked Dawn, remembering her own parents' destructive obsession and Logan's lethal skill at poker.

"No. Logan hasn't played for money since he won the Lazy W from your dad." She saw Dawn's surprised look and nodded. "Yeah. Not once. He told me that it was a start on Joe's revenge and that was all he'd ever wanted."

"Vengeance," breathed Dawn, feeling a chill move over her.

"Don't look like that," pleaded Kathy, taking Dawn's cold hand in her own. "It's over and done with. He's not out for vengeance anymore. He's—oh, Dawn, he's killing himself," she said in a rush. "The doctor says he has pneumonia, but Logan won't stop working. He looks like hell. Dr. Martin gave up on him and Logan won't listen to me anymore. He won't listen to anyone. He doesn't let anyone come close except the twins. He loves them so much it makes me cry to watch."

Kathy's hands tightened around Dawn's, as though touch could say more than words. "He should have his own family and a woman to take care of him," said Kathy. "Then he'd have something to live for besides a bunch of dumb white-faced cows that don't give a damn about him!"

Dawn closed her eyes, afraid that their green depths would reveal how very much she had once wanted to be the woman Logan cared about, the woman who would give him children, the woman who would weave herself sweetly, deeply, into the pattern of his life.

"Logan is old enough to find a woman if that's what he wants," Dawn said clearly, her voice very controlled as she opened her eyes again.

"Not likely," said Kathy. "Since he won the Lazy W, he's been hell on wheels. He's harder than ever, even more determined not to give anything to a woman. Oh, from time to time he uses them sure enough. But marriage and a family? No way. Not even affairs. And lonely? God, yes, he's lonely. It's eating him alive, and he doesn't even have booze to numb the pain. He'll never admit that he's lonely and hurting, though. Not even to himself."

Blindly Dawn looked toward the empty loom that dominated the tiny cabin. Logan was continuing the pattern that had begun so long ago. Hatred and revenge, destruction and loneliness—the very things that had driven her away three years ago.

"I can't," Dawn said softly, fighting to keep her voice level.

There was a long silence before Kathy sighed. "I didn't want to have to do it this way," she said, "but now I don't have any choice. You say you owe me because of that $5,000 I gave you three years ago."

"*You*, yes. Logan, no."

"It wasn't my money," said Kathy in a rush. "Logan gave it to me and told me to give it to you for a new start somewhere else and to say that I got the money from my savings account."

Dawn stared at Kathy as though she had never seen the other woman. "What? What are you saying?"

"Your debt isn't to me," Kathy said bluntly. "It's to Logan. It was his idea, his money. He gave you a break three years ago. Now he needs one, and you can give it to him."

Dawn sat for a long, silent moment, her eyes brooding over the waiting loom, her hands held so tightly that they ached. The past whirled around her, its familiar bleak pattern changed by a few words.

Three years ago Logan cared enough about me to see that I wasn't left penniless after Dad lost the ranch. Logan asked nothing of me in return, not even the knowledge that he was the one who had helped me when I had no one to turn to.

Now he needs help, whether he knows it or not. Kathy isn't a fool. She wouldn't be here if things weren't desperate.

"Why me?" asked Dawn finally, her voice that of a stranger.

"We've tried nurses and housekeepers," admitted Kathy. "They never lasted more than a few days. They took it personally when Logan cussed them out."

"I see." Dawn swallowed. "How about the foreman?"

"He quit. Logan broke his nose."

"Oh." She gave Kathy a long look. "What makes you think I'll have any better luck?"

"Logan never had any use for people outside his family. Especially Sheridans. But he gave you that $5,000."

Dawn saw the curiosity in Kathy's gaze, the question that hadn't been asked three years ago and wouldn't be asked now. Or answered.

"Perhaps he felt guilty about taking the Lazy W from my parents," offered Dawn.

Kathy's laugh was rather like Logan's—short and humorless. "Logan could have killed your mother and never looked back. For him guilt is a dictionary word somewhere between guile and gutless." She sighed. "Dawn, if I had anywhere else to turn, I would. I don't know what happened three years ago between you two. When I left for college after spring break, nothing was wrong. A week later Logan shows up, hands me five thousand dollars and tells me to give it to you. I did. I didn't ask why then and I'm not asking now. I'm just telling you that Logan is killing himself. What you do about it is up to you."

Dawn sat without moving for a long time, remembering too many unhappy things. *I wasn't strong enough to stand up to Logan three years ago. Am I strong enough to go back and face him now?*

Then Dawn realized that the question was meaningless. She had taken from Logan without realizing it and had given nothing in return.

Strong or weak, ready or not, she had to go back to him.

Two

The road to the Lazy W wound between white banks created by the snowplow's broad blade. The sun on the road kept the black surface free of ice during the late morning and early afternoon. Beyond that, driving was dicey. Dawn was used to it. She knew that ice lurked on the northern exposures and along shaded curves. She knew that bridges froze earlier and thawed later than macadam. She also knew that her little Volkswagen bug with its rear engine was a better snow car than it looked.

It didn't, however, have four-wheel drive. There were stretches of ranch road where she bounced from rut to snowy rut, hanging on to the wheel with all the strength in her five-foot-five-inch body. In some ways she almost welcomed the rough patches. They kept her mind off the knowledge that Logan Garrett lived at the end of the road to the Lazy W. They kept memories from overwhelming her as she came closer and closer to what once had been her home.

Why hadn't Logan stayed at his other ranch? Why had he moved to the Lazy W and let Kathy's husband run the Garrett ranch?

It would have been easier to confront Logan somewhere else. Here every rock and snowbank reminded her of her childhood and of the tangled history of the Garrett and Sheridan families. Not for the first time in her life, Dawn devoutly wished that her mother had been a different sort of woman. Then Mary Sue wouldn't have jilted Joe Garrett in order to marry Sonny Sheridan, the spoiled child of wealthy ranchers. Mary Sue had been a poor girl from Kentucky. She had wanted the biggest ranch in a hundred miles and had married Sonny to get it. Sonny had wanted a woman who matched him in wildness and in gambling lust. Both Mary Sue and Sonny had gotten what they wanted. Ultimately, it had destroyed them.

It had destroyed Joe Garrett, too. He had never gotten over being left at the church by Mary Sue O'Hara. By the time he had given up and gone back to his small ranch, Mary Sue's name was Sheridan and she and Sonny were spending their honeymoon in the casinos of Las Vegas. Joe was spending what would have been his honeymoon in the bottom of a bottle, cursing Mary Sue terribly, trying to drown the humiliation of being dumped for a man whose only attraction was a big ranch. That had been the beginning of two patterns that would repeat over and over again—her parents' obsession with gambling and Joe's obsession with whiskey.

Dawn dragged her thoughts away from the past. For a mile or so she talked to Prowl, who sat in disgruntled splendor amid the huge plastic bags of yarn that were stuffed into the back seat. The cat's only response to Dawn's

conversational gambit was a dirty look and a waspish twitch
of her long tail.

Sighing, Dawn went back to her own thoughts, and her
thoughts went back to the past.

*What had Joe Garrett looked like? What had he been like
before he loved the wrong woman? Had he been big and
lean and fast like Logan? Did he have the same tawny brown
hair and nearly gold eyes?*

Dawn's memories gave her no answers. She had never
seen Logan's brother. She had grown up knowing about Joe
and Mary Sue and Sonny the way a child knows about sea-
sons—she had simply absorbed the facts without question.
Even at eighteen Dawn hadn't questioned the assertion that
her mother had been responsible for the ruin of a fine young
man.

Now, for the first time in her life, Dawn was becoming
curious about that "fine young man" who had died when
she was twelve. Logan had been twenty. Joe had been—
what? Thirty-eight? He had been so much older than Kathy
and Logan that Joe had been more father than brother to
them. Other than his age, his love-hate for Mary Sue, and
his terminal alcoholism, Dawn knew little about the man
whose life and death were part of the very warp of her
childhood.

There was one thing she knew about Joe Garrett. As a
child, Logan had all but worshiped Joe. As a young man,
Logan had done everything he could to take care of the
much older brother who wouldn't take care of himself. It
was a pattern Dawn had seen repeated in one of her school-
mates, a girl who was fiercely protective of her hard-
drinking father. The parent-child roles had been reversed,
often with unhappy results. For then the child felt responsible for the parent's drinking. Rather than confront the
human weakness of the parent, the child blamed himself or

bad luck or bad companions, anything but the person who lifted the glass to his lips and drank.

Had Logan been like that, protecting Joe rather than confronting his alcoholism?

Dawn rolled down the window and let the chill sweet air wash over her, blowing away unhappy memories and speculations. She couldn't see the high peaks that ringed the long, rolling valley, for clouds had lowered over the mountains, shrouding them halfway down their forested flanks. On the southern exposures the snow had partially melted, revealing earth that was almost black. In a few weeks new grass would appear—scattered shadows of translucent-green, the first frail intimations of spring. Then the white-faced cattle would nibble eagerly on the tender green, grazing with their muscular backs to the April wind.

But in March there was only snow and rock, ice and gray clouds. Spring was coming, though. The cows knew it. Their certainty was revealed beneath their thick winter coats in bodies bulging with the promise of spring calves.

"You're going to have your hands full," Dawn muttered to herself. "Calves are going to start coming within a few weeks. Better pray no spring blizzard comes with them."

Prowl's cold nose bumped against Dawn's ear, distracting her.

"Want out, girl?" asked Dawn.

The cat sniffed the rich scents pouring in through the window before she turned and went back to her nest among the heaped bags of yarn. All Prowl wanted was an end to the ride.

Dawn drove the last miles through the rolling valley in silence, letting the scents and sights of her lost home break over her in an endless, silent wave. She hadn't realized how much she had missed the Lazy W until that instant. Tears she couldn't stop made her cheeks first hot, then cold.

"I can't face Logan like this," she said, wiping her eyes with the bright sleeve of her woven-wool coat, trying to bring herself back under control. It didn't work.

Dawn stopped the car, got out and plunged her hands into a snowbank. She scrubbed her face until her cheeks were red. The shock of the snow drove away her tears. An effort of will drove away the memories. Firmly she reminded herself that her parents lived in Florida now, and her grandmother was dead. Dawn wasn't driving back down a road that led to the haunting, frightening past. Nor was she coming home. She was paying off a debt, period. When nothing more was owed she would go back to Aspen and pray very hard that Logan Garrett's eyes and touch would no longer haunt her dreams.

With renewed determination Dawn got back in the car and drove up to the house. There was an aura of disintegration about it that made her wonder if Logan had left it empty for three years and just recently moved in. Several of the shutters were subtly askew, telling her that the living room would have icy drafts when the northern wind blew. The flower beds she had tended so carefully along the front of the house were thick with the dried, snow-flattened husks of last summer's weeds. The rose bushes she had loved looked as though they hadn't been touched since the morning she had packed her suitcase and fled from Logan Garrett's sensuous touch and cynical eyes.

"Don't get too comfortable, Prowl," she told the cat, who was sniffing at a hole beneath the wooden porch steps with great interest. "I think Kathy was wrong. Logan doesn't live here. No one does."

As if to prove Dawn correct, no one came when she knocked at the front door. She called out. No one answered. Shrugging, she opened the door. It was hard to feel like a trespasser in what had once been her own home.

A small sound escaped Dawn's lips when she saw the living room. Someone lived there all right—the way a pig lived in a pen. Two muddy jackets and several pairs of equally muddy boots were strewn randomly about. The beautiful Navajo rugs on the floor were all but invisible beneath a coating of mud. The couch with the soft blue-green cover she had woven was now the color of bread mold. The curtains were gone. The family photos were gone. The bouquets of dried herbs and flowers that she had made to brighten the long winter nights were gone. Nothing was in their place but a thick layer of dust.

The kitchen was a disaster.

Appalled, Dawn's green eyes widened as she took in the piles of dirty dishes, a stove coated with grease, countertops where bold mice had left footprints and other less appetizing signs in the grime, and a floor that was slightly less clean than the engine compartment of her car. Food in various stages of decay crusted the surface of every pan and plate in sight.

Prowl leaped up onto the countertop and began sniffing the mouse trails with electric interest.

"Bon appetit," muttered Dawn, wishing Prowl were twins—or triplets.

She spun on her heel, marched into the living room and picked up the phone. To her surprise a dial tone greeted her. She dialed Kathy's number and waited for five rings.

"Hi, Kathy," said Dawn. Her voice was confident, relieved. She wouldn't have to confront Logan right away. She had been sent to the wrong place.

"You sure sound cheerful. You at the Lazy W?" Kathy asked dubiously.

"Uh-huh. I don't know who's living here right now, but it isn't Logan," said Dawn. "He has his shortcomings, but terminal slobbishness isn't one of them."

Kathy's sigh was long and heavy. "I told you, Dawn. He's been sick. Most nights I'll bet he's so tired when he comes in he doesn't even eat. He won't let anyone help him. He wouldn't even let me inside when I was there at Christmas. Told me to get my butt back to my husband where I belonged."

Dawn's only answer was a long silence. Then she asked, "Just how long has Logan been living here?"

"Since you left."

Silence.

"Dawn?"

More silence, followed by the words, "How long would it take you to get a cleaning crew up here?"

"Tried that," said Kathy laconically.

"And?"

"See that shotgun hanging over the front door?"

Dawn turned and looked. She should have noticed the gun before. It was the only clean thing in the whole house. "Yes."

"Rock salt. The crew took one round of it in their jeans and lit out. Can't say as I blame them."

"Are you sure Logan isn't drinking?" demanded Dawn.

"Do you see any bottles?" asked Kathy, her voice suddenly anxious.

"No. Every other damn thing," she said in disgust, "but no bottles."

"Then he's not drinking," said Kathy succinctly. "Joe left bottles all over the place."

Dawn closed her eyes. All around her was the lair of a man who simply didn't care anymore. That wasn't like Logan. He had cared intensely. Wrongly, perhaps, but intensely. "Kathy, what happened to Logan?"

"I don't think revenge agreed with him," said Kathy simply.

"Either that," said Dawn, her voice grim, "or he's still taking out his hatred for my mother on the ranch she wanted more than she wanted Joe Garrett."

"Does the land look mistreated? Or the cows?"

"No. Just the house and the gardens."

"Figures. From what I hear, Mary Sue was big on curtains, flowers and giving orders to the hands."

Dawn balled her fingers into a fist and wanted to weep. What if the neglected house represented contempt rather than a simple lack of caring? And if that were true, what would Logan do when he saw her, Mary Sue's daughter?

"Kathy, do you really know what you're asking me to do?" she asked hoarsely. *"Logan hates me."*

"I'm betting he doesn't," said Kathy. "I'm betting he'd love you if you gave him half a chance."

"You are crazy," said Dawn, spacing each word with extreme care.

"Maybe. Maybe not. Eight weeks, Dawn. Then you can run again and never look back. Or you can stay and marry Logan and have his kids, which is what should have developed the last time I threw the two of you together three years ago!"

There was a very long silence.

"Dawn?" asked Kathy softly. "You still there?"

"Yes," she whispered.

"Somewhere underneath all that anger is a good man. Find him, honey. Bring him home to all of us."

Long after Kathy had hung up, Dawn stood and stared at the phone, letting the knowledge of just how completely she had been manipulated sink in. Kathy thought that Logan needed a woman. Kathy provided one, dusted off her hands and headed for the hills until the bloodshed was over.

From the kitchen came a clatter and a crash, followed by Prowl's triumphant yeow-yeow-yeow! For cat and mouse, the bloodshed had already begun. With a grimace Dawn went to the living-room door and held it open. A few seconds later Prowl strutted by. Dawn was careful not to look too closely at the limp form dangling from the cat's mouth.

Dawn knew exactly how the greedy mouse felt.

The thought was not comfortable. Neither was the next one: *What if Kathy is right? What if Logan could learn to love me?*

And if pigs could fly they'd be eagles, Dawn reminded herself grimly, squelching the stubborn hope that had always been woven like an incandescent thread through her dark memories of Logan Garrett. She had better concentrate on the most likely pattern—Kathy was telling herself sweet lies in order to ease her conscience for trapping her friend into what could be the worst eight weeks of her life.

Restlessly Dawn looked around the living room. The big muddy boots and jackets stared back at her as though to underline the massive contempt of their owner for her.

Yet Logan was the only man who had ever gotten past her fear of herself, sensuality and men. He had made her feel beautiful, capable of love—

And humiliated to her soul.

Yet no matter how often Dawn reminded herself how it had ended in shame, she could neither forget nor deny the ravishing beauty of being undressed by Logan, seeing desire ignite in his eyes, feeling the shocking perfection of his mouth caressing her breast. Heat had raced through her, shaking her until she trembled helplessly and he had smiled and said, *Hold on to me, little leaf. The storm is just beginning.*

With a small sound Dawn forced her mind away from the image of herself shivering within Logan's powerful arms. Her own potential for passion and sensuality horrified her. If there was any one thing she should have learned from the past, it was that passion and men were a source of destruction and despair. The fact that Mary Sue had passed on to her daughter that same quality of elegant, elemental sensual challenge terrified Dawn when she was forced to confront it in a man's eyes. The day she had looked into the mirror and had seen her mother staring back at her was the day Dawn had sworn she would never let passion control her. And she hadn't.

Until Logan Garrett had touched her and she had felt her body turn to fire.

Almost frantically Dawn looked around the living room, suddenly seeing the whole house as a cage from which she couldn't escape for fifty-six days. The thought made her heart race wildly. She took a deep breath and called calmness to herself the way her grandmother had taught her so long ago. *Face what you fear. Learn its pattern. Learn to weave yourself into the pattern rather than rail against it.*

Yes. The house was a cage. But even the wildest creature could survive eight weeks in a cage if the animal had sense enough not to beat itself to death against the bars.

Dawn's tightly held breath came out in a long sigh. She looked around the room again. She could tolerate a cage if she had to—but she'd be damned if she'd wade through filth while she marked off the days. With a final look around, she peeled off her coat and got to work.

The cleaning supplies were where she expected them to be, on the back porch. The storm windows that made the porch weather-tight looked as though they hadn't been washed by anything but the rain in years. From the appearance of the buckets, nothing except mice had used them since Dawn had left. With determined motions she plugged both of the deep, oversize utility sinks, filled them with scalding water, bleach and detergent, and began carrying crusty pots and plates from kitchen to porch. When the sinks finally were full, the kitchen surfaces were fully revealed for the first time. Dawn muttered a few words she rarely used and decided to fill the washing machine before she took on the kitchen counters.

The upstairs bedrooms were even more bleak than the living room. A wall had been taken out between two of the bedrooms, creating a master suite. Pieces of plaster still littered the floor along with tufts of insulation and random nails. A king-size bed had replaced the smaller one her parents had used. A beautifully carved, very dusty folding screen divided the room where the wall had once been.

Dawn took one look at the sheets and decided that Logan had taken to sleeping with his boots on. She picked up a clot of mud and flung it to the floor. With quick jerks she stripped every bit of the bedding and hauled it to the downstairs porch where the washer and dryer were. She poked tentatively among the soaking dishes, decided that they needed more time and went to the kitchen with a bucket in one hand and a scrub brush in the other. She ignored the floor—right now she wasn't concerned about anything she wasn't going to eat from or cook on. When the bucket was filled with a hot, caustic combination of bleach and detergent, Dawn began scrubbing the kitchen counters.

By the third bucket she could see the familiar pattern of the Spanish tile gleaming through. The scarlet flowers had always reminded her of fireweed, the first plant to grow on burned areas. That wildflower was her favorite plant, for not only was it elegant and resilient, it also prepared the way for the less hardy plants that followed. Without fireweed the landscape would have looked scarred and desolate. With it the land was both beautiful and fertile.

When there was one truly clean surface, Dawn began to think of dinner. A trip to the refrigerator and cupboards rewarded her with a carton of milk that was no longer liquid and an array of canned goods that could hardly be described as mouthwatering. The only thing that had survived in the refrigerator was a big ceramic pot of ghastly looking, darkly fermenting goo, which she recognized as sourdough starter gone feral. There was no doubt of its yeastiness, though. Or its sourness.

"My God," said Dawn, already planning what she was going to say to Logan about his slovenly housekeeping. "I don't need a bucket and brush for this kitchen," she muttered. "I need a whip and a chair!"

She reamed out the coffeepot, found a can of coffee on its side behind a pile of baked-bean cans and made coffee to fortify herself. The smell of it revived her enough to tackle the revolting looking but eminently usable sourdough starter.

A short time later Dawn set aside a mound of bread dough to rise, covering it with a clean napkin she had taken from her own car, and tackled the freezer. There was plenty of beef. She pulled out something labeled sirloin steak, unwrapped it and decided that she'd never seen such an advanced case of freezer burn.

"Stew or soup, Dawn," she muttered. "Which will it be?" She hesitated as she weighed the unappealing meat. "Right. Soup. And don't skimp on the herbs and garlic."

She couldn't find a clean pot that was big enough for the bedraggled steak. Muttering, she went back out on the porch and poked around in one of the sinks until she had fished out a sizable pot. She didn't speculate on what it once might have held. She just scraped and cleaned until there was nothing left but shining metal on the inside. Ignoring the generous layers of carbonized grease that decorated the stove, she slammed the pot onto a big burner and turned the flame to high. She added water, steak, and herbs that had belonged to her grandmother. From the looks of the tins and jars containing the herbs, no one had used them since the day Mary Sue had walked out of the house with the single suitcase that Logan had allowed her.

Prowl yowled imperiously in front of a floor-level cupboard door. Dawn opened that door and then every other one at floor level. The cat flowed into the cupboard. A few instants later there was a crash and a mad invisible scramble beneath the countertop. Other than leaving the back porch door ajar for Prowl's eventual triumphant exit, Dawn ignored the cat. It was easier that way.

By the time the soup was simmering, the washing machine was ready for a new load. It didn't take Dawn long to find one. She just went to Logan's bedroom, picked up everything that wasn't metal, wood or leather, and held her breath until she could dump the lot into the washing machine. Then she scrubbed plates and silverware and glasses until it was time to knock down the bread dough and let it rise again. The rest of the afternoon passed that way, going from stove to sinks to washing machine and back again, with time out for a run at the kitchen table and refrigerator for the sake of variety.

The one thing Dawn didn't do was unpack her Volkswagen or wash a set of sheets for her own use on one of the upstairs beds. When she realized that, she realized that she wasn't sure she was going to stay. Not for eight weeks. Probably not even for a single night. As she had worked over the house, the pattern had become painfully clear: the man who lived here wasn't the Logan Garrett she remembered. Three years ago he had been careful of himself and his surroundings. He hadn't been afraid of dirt—but he hadn't wallowed in it, either.

By late afternoon the smell of freshly baked bread permeated the house, bringing a heady feeling of warmth and homecoming with it. Dawn stretched her tired back, feeling the past hours in every protesting muscle. Her hands were aching and nearly raw from the cleaning solvents she had used. If she didn't look at the floor or the stove, the kitchen was clean. So was everything in the cupboards, which Prowl had rid of resident mice. On the counter was a grocery list that covered two sheets of lined paper. Before she left she would see that the pantry and freezer were stocked with palatable foods.

Before she left . . .

Dawn heard the thought echo and knew that it was true. She had to leave. She saw the pattern too clearly to stay. Logan had changed too much. Everything she had seen in the house shouted that Logan had made his choices, set his pattern and would follow it to its bleak conclusion. Like his brother before him, Logan was a man who had cut himself off from everything that was gentle, elegant, creative . . . feminine.

The Dawn Sheridan of today might have been strong enough to take on the Logan Garrett of three years ago. She wasn't strong enough to survive a head-on confrontation with today's Logan Garrett, however. If Logan discovered the gentleness in her he would destroy her. And if she stayed he would discover that gentleness as inevitably as sunrise discovered the mountain peaks.

"I'm sorry, Kathy," murmured Dawn, staring at her work-reddened hands. "You looked at your brother through the eyes of love and thought that was what he wanted. Love. Not quite, my friend. Not quite. Logan wanted vengeance for Joe's death. He still wants it."

Dawn braced her knuckles against the small of her back and dug in hard. She was still working on the knotted muscles when she heard a pickup truck pull into the front yard. It seemed a very long time before she heard the truck door slam and the sound of booted feet climbing up onto the front porch. The sounds were oddly erratic, almost tentative. So were the small noises he made as he fumbled over opening the front door.

Dawn hurried through the living room, wondering if she had somehow locked the front door on one of her trips to the Volkswagen. She opened the door.

"Logan?" she asked, unable to believe that he was the man leaning against the doorframe.

She had forgotten how big he was. Even slouching, he towered over her. His shoulders were as wide as the door. His clothes were too loose, as though he had borrowed them from an even larger man. He hadn't shaved in days—brown stubble grew thickly on his face. The rest of his hair was a very dark bronze and curiously lifeless. His skin was as pale as salt beneath the weathered tan. Sweat stood on his forehead and left wet trails over his cheekbones. Amber eyes tried to focus on her.

"Dawn?" Logan asked, his voice harsh, disbelieving.

His hand shook visibly when he tried to touch her cheek as though to prove to himself that she was real. His fingers missed their target, brushing air instead. He shook his head, trying to clear it. His hat bumped against the doorframe and fell off. He didn't notice. His eyes were glazed and his body swayed. With an enormous effort he gathered himself enough to lurch into the room and onto the couch. He fell back across the dirty cushions and did not move again.

"Logan!"

Dawn flew across the room and knelt beside Logan. She held her breath, expecting a stench of stale alcohol to repel her. There was no reek of whiskey on his breath or body. Tentatively she touched his cheek.

Hot. Hot enough to burn.

"Dear God," she breathed.

Kathy had been right. Logan was too sick to look after himself—and too proud and stubborn to let anyone help.

Dawn left Logan long enough to retrieve the quilt she had just washed and dried. She tucked it firmly around his body. A trip to the bathroom netted her an unused bottle of prescription antibiotics and a tin of aspirin. She got a glass of water and returned to Logan. She coaxed him into a sitting position, put the antibiotic in his mouth and held the glass to his lips. He swallowed automatically.

"Dawn?" he said, his eyes not quite focused. "No... dreaming..."

"Yes," she soothed, instinctively knowing that he wouldn't want her to see him like this. "Just a dream."

She gave him the aspirin, reassured him again that he was dreaming and held her breath. He slipped into a restless kind of unconsciousness that was stilled only when she put her hand on his hair and stroked with slow, reassuring motions. Then he sighed, turned his cheek into her palm and slept deeply.

Blinded by her own tears, Dawn didn't see the cage door closing behind her.

Three

———

The first light of day filtered through the uncurtained, unwashed windows of the living room. Logan stirred randomly, neither asleep nor quite awake, held in the halfway house of the mind where memories are relived as vividly as dreams. The images that came to him were bits of the past, and their only connecting link was the haunted green eyes of Dawn Sheridan watching him.

Logan turned restlessly on the old couch, trying to evade the memories. It didn't do any good. This morning he could no more deny his memories than he could deny the sunlight flooding through the windows. . . .

"C'mon, Logan," said Kathy, half pleading, half demanding. "You know it isn't fair to blame Dawn for what Mary Sue did to Joe."

Logan bit off a curse and ran his large hand through his hair, wondering how he could agree with Kathy and still not

have to put up with seeing the sad-eyed, thin waif who had
haunted him since Kathy had first brought Dawn Sheridan
home years ago. It wasn't that he blamed Dawn for Joe's
death. It was simply that seeing her was a constant reminder of the helpless pain Logan had endured watching
Joe's descent into alcoholic purgatory and death—all for a
woman who wasn't worth the powder it would take to blow
her to hell.

"Kathleen," Logan began carefully, searching for words
to make his younger sister understand what it cost for him
to have Mary Sue's daughter around.

Kathy groaned aloud, interrupting him. "Whenever you
use my full name you're trying to say no. Logan, I'm not
asking you to give back the ranch you won last night, or the
house, or the furniture or even the clothes you'll never use."
Kathy put her hand on her brother's sleeve and looked up
at him appealingly. "It's just that Dawn doesn't have anyone since her grandma died and I went away to college."

"She has her parents," said Logan in a clipped voice.

"With help like that," retorted Kathy, "it's a wonder she
survived childhood."

Logan swore briefly, savagely. "I didn't mean for Dawn
to be hurt," he said in a harsh voice. "I made it very clear
to Mary Sue that Dawn should take every bit of what was
hers from the house."

Grimly Logan tried not to visualize a frail, big-eyed child
with a suitcase in each hand and nowhere to go. He told
himself coldly that Dawn was eighteen now, legally responsible for her own life, more than capable of supporting herself. Hell, at eighteen his own mother had had a child and
was running a ranch while her husband worked in town. But
Logan didn't really believe in Dawn's maturity. He hadn't
seen Dawn up close since she was fifteen, and then she had
looked more like twelve. In his mind she was still a child and

as such she should be protected from the harshest of life's blows.

Including Logan Garrett's revenge.

"Damnation!" he grated, giving up. "You win, Kath. Invite her here for spring vacation. If it works out, she can live here while she finishes high school."

"What about college for her?" persisted Kathy. "She's very bright, Logan. She sees things about people and feelings that are...well, darned scary, sometimes. It's like she's eighty, not eighteen. For the past few years she's practically run the ranch for her fool father. It isn't fair that she should have to spend her life slinging hash for drunks just because her parents lost an all-night poker match with you."

"You'd defend Dawn as if she was dumb as a stump," retorted Logan.

"Yeah," conceded Kathy, smiling. "But she isn't. Dawn's as smart as you, big brother. Smarter, when it comes to people. She's had to be to survive."

"All right, all right!" he said, throwing up his hands in mock surrender. Then he grinned. "Bring your little friend home, Kathy. If she's as bright as you say, I'll work out something for her education. Okay?"

"Okay!" said Kathy, throwing her arms around him and kissing his cheek noisily....

Logan rolled over restlessly on the couch, not wanting the memories to continue, not wanting to know again the shock and hurt in Dawn's beautiful eyes. But the memories came inevitably, relentlessly, like drops of water melting from a glacier, drops running together to make a pure, agonizingly cold stream....

Logan heard Kathy's excited voice even before she opened the front door.

"You can share my room until I go back to college in a few weeks. Then you can stay here and finish high school. You won't have to go to Vegas with your parents."

"Kathy, you don't have to do this. That poker game was fair. Everyone knows that Logan is as honest as a winter wind."

Logan had been walking toward the front door, reaching out to open it; but Dawn's voice stopped his body, his hand, his heart. She had the most exquisitely beautiful voice he had ever heard. Low, gentle, rich with muted emotion. Like Mary Sue's. Only Mary Sue's voice had never held this much subtlety, this much music. Mary Sue's tones had been husky, haunting, infinitely alluring, promising what the woman herself had never delivered—undying passion. Dawn's voice promised, too, but it would take a lifetime to discover and number the promises.

And each one of them would be a lie, Logan reminded himself grimly, remembering Joe's lingering, lonely death.

With a feeling of growing coldness Logan opened the front door. Dawn turned at the sound, looking up at him from beneath lashes as long and thick as midnight. In that instant he felt as though he had taken a paralyzing body blow. For the first time in his life he understood—really understood—why his brother had drunk himself to death over a woman he could never have.

"Mary Sue?"

But the elegant, sensual creature on his doorstep wasn't Mary Sue Sheridan. It was Dawn. Oh, the eyes were the same—green gems set off by skin that made a pearl look rough. But Dawn's eyes were deep, almost serene, where Mary Sue's had held a brittle sexual challenge that few men could ignore. The raven silk of Dawn's hair was the same as her mother's, but instead of being enticingly free, the hair was bound in a single French braid that reached to Dawn's waist. And a slender waist it was. The rest of her body was the same. Slim, almost delicate, as sensual and elegant as a cat. Mary Sue had been the same. Sleek rather than voluptuous. Yet somehow her body had been as sexy and challenging as the stirring in a man's loins when he watched her walk by.

Graceful as a cat. And like a cat, cruel.

Logan heard in his mind Mary Sue's last raging words before she walked away from the poker game that had cost her the Lazy W: *I'll get even, Logan Garrett, if it's the last thing I do!* Was that why Dawn was here? Revenge? Had Mary Sue sent her daughter here to twist his guts into knots and then hang him with them?

The almost shy smile on Dawn's lips faded, telling Logan exactly how hard his own expression must be. He stepped back stiffly, wordlessly inviting Dawn inside. Then he gave Kathy a look that promised retribution as he remembered his blithe words: *Bring your little friend home.* Kathy had done nothing to correct his impression that Dawn was still the same thin, shy preadolescent who had looked twelve when she was fifteen—the same fragile child who had watched Logan chop wood and brand cattle as though he were the most fascinating creature in the world.

"I'm Dawn, Mr. Garrett," she said, stepping into the living room and instantly standing to one side, as though she were a half-tame animal that didn't want to get too far from the door.

"So you are," he said, looking at her from the crown of her head to her slender feet. "You look like your mother, little girl," he drawled, his voice subtly provocative.

Dawn gave him a swift, almost stricken glance, then said so quietly that he had to strain to hear, "That's what people tell me."

It was Kathy who got them over the next awkward moments. It was Kathy who kept up a determined conversation over dinner, trying to display Dawn's intelligence and running smack into Dawn's deepening silence. Logan had watched his sister and Dawn and the disintegrating evening with almost amused detachment. He didn't have to be convinced that Dawn was quick when it came to people. She had taken one look at him and known that he wanted her. He wanted to strip off her clothes and taste for himself the sensual excitement that shimmered beneath her serene exterior. He wanted to know how it would feel to bury himself in that sleek feminine body and wring the last drop of passion from her shivering flesh.

Yes, Logan told himself silently, savagely. *Dawn knows what I'm thinking. And she's frightened. Had Mary Sue been like that? Had she been frightened by Joe's honest sexuality? Was that why she had slept with every damn man in Colorado but Joe?*

Well, it won't be like that with Dawn. She'll sleep with me and no other man for as long as I want her. She'll be the one to learn what it's like to be wholly dependent on another person for your happiness and to have that person coolly, cruelly walk all over your pride until nothing is left, not even a will to live.

But she wouldn't know that. Not until it was too late. . . .

Half-asleep, yet too awake, Logan groaned softly and put his powerful forearm over his eyes as though that would block out the memories as well as the sunlight pouring into the ruined living room of the Lazy W ranch house. The sunrise was dimmed by his arm. The memories flowed on unhindered, melting from the frigid past, each image and phrase another icy freshet joining the glacial river of revenge and regret. . . .

Logan waited for dinner to be over with a raging impatience that was almost beyond his ability to conceal. Almost but not quite. The past few weeks had taught him the kind of patience he hadn't known he had in him. He had stalked Dawn more carefully than a winter-starved wolf stalking a fawn. He had permitted nothing of his own hunger to show. He had treated her casually while Kathy was there, ignoring Dawn more often than not. And when he couldn't ignore her without being rude, he treated her as though she were still twelve.

Even so, it had taken a week for Dawn to get over her obvious uneasiness with Logan. The second week had been a gentle torment, for Dawn had slowly begun to smile at him again, to watch him with large green eyes every time he moved, to look from his hair to his lips and then to his hands, as though wondering about him in the way a woman wonders about a man she wants.

Logan couldn't believe that Dawn was as naive about men as she sometimes seemed. After a time he decided that it didn't matter. If she was an experienced actress, he could control her with the Lazy W as Mary Sue's husband had ultimately controlled his wife. If Dawn were inexperienced, he could use her own undiscovered sensuality to control her. Either way he would be safe—unlike Joe, who hadn't understood what Mary Sue was until it was far too late and he was irrevocably in love with a bitch who cut out his heart and traded it for the Lazy W. But it wasn't Joe's fault he hadn't loved wisely. He hadn't had an older brother to watch and learn from. Logan had.

By the third week of Dawn's stay, Kathy had been gone. Each night Logan had resisted the hot urgings of his body. Instead of pulling Dawn into his arms and kissing her senseless, he had talked with her about the Lazy W, and he had been surprised by the extent of her knowledge. It had become clear to him that she loved the land deeply, and that she knew it better than any hired hand. She knew which valleys would grow loco weed before other natural feed came in. She knew which of the seven creeks flooded and under what conditions those floods endangered cattle. She knew precisely how many cattle her father had run. She knew which cows were barren and which dropped twins. Yet not once had Dawn expressed any resentment over losing the Lazy W to Logan Garrett, nor had she asked to remain on the ranch. She had asked about him, though, and she had listened to every answer with vivid attention.

Logan put the thought out of his mind with an impatient curse. Perhaps she was simply a better actress than he believed anyone could be. Not that it mattered. He had had her within reach for nearly a month. He wasn't going to wait any longer. The next time those luminous green eyes looked from his mouth to his hands, he would answer her silent questions.

He looked up from his plate and saw her watching him. Very carefully he set aside his fork. With unconscious, feline grace Dawn stood and began to clear the table.

"You don't have to do that," said Logan. "You cooked. I'll clean up. That's the deal Kathy and I always had after the cook quit."

Dawn looked up at him through a tangle of thick black lashes. "It's the least I can do, Logan. No, please," she said quickly, touching his arm. "I used to do it all the time at home."

"You like doing dishes?" he asked skeptically, ignoring the sudden hard slam of his heart when he felt her fingertips against the naked skin of his forearm.

Her brief smile was like a caress. "No, but I like thinking about the next tapestry I'm going to weave, and I think better when my hands are busy."

It was a physical effort for Logan not to suggest a more interesting way for Dawn to keep her hands busy. With a silent curse he went into the living room and stirred up the logs until the flames licked hotly against the dark opening of the flue. The clock said that only fifteen minutes had passed until Dawn joined him in the living room for the after-dinner talk that had become the unacknowledged highlight of his day. It seemed more like fifteen hours.

"No late blizzards forecast?" asked Dawn, setting Logan's coffee on the low table in front of the couch.

Logan shook his head even as he realized that he had forgotten to turn on the TV and check the cable channel that provided continuous news of interest to ranchers. His forgetfulness shocked him. Considering that his entire crop of spring calves was dependent on decent weather, it was unbelievable that he hadn't given even a thought to Colorado's treacherous tendency to freeze solid in the midst of spring's most melting promises.

Silently he sipped at the fiercely hot black coffee that Dawn had so quickly learned to make for him. For a moment he became lost in speculation about what other, much hotter, things he could teach her.

"Logan?"

He blinked and focused on Dawn. Her fingers were on his forearm again, and her spring-green eyes were watching first his eyes, then his lips. "Yes?" he murmured.

It was Dawn's turn not to answer. She didn't have to. Logan could see the sensual questions in her luminous, almost frightened eyes. Without looking away from her, he set aside his coffee cup.

"Yes," he said softly, and he bent over her lips, answering her unasked questions.

The first touch of his mouth on hers told Logan that Dawn hadn't been acting the part of a shy maiden. She was as green as meadow grass when it came to sex. The knowledge gave Logan a deep, unexpected thrill of triumph...and a contradictory stirring of tenderness. For an instant he asked himself if he had any right to take what Dawn was offering. Then he remembered that this was Mary Sue's daughter, incapable of real love. But not of passion. So he would take Mary Sue's daughter and bind her irrevocably in sensual chains; but he would do it sweetly, delicately, leading Dawn so gently into the trap that she would never know what had happened until he held her helpless in the palm of his hand.

Logan kissed Dawn as though she were as fragile as the first wildflower blooming through a bank of snow. He felt the hand on his forearm tighten until her fingers must have ached. Smiling, he rubbed his lips lightly over hers, letting her feel the warmth of his breath and his fingertips as he touched her cheek. Her black lashes lifted, revealing to him the jeweled green of her eyes. He didn't even realize that he had closed his arms around her and lifted her into his lap until he heard her breathless protest.

"Hush, little darling," he murmured, dropping kisses around the curving lines of her mouth, loosening the powerful pressure of his arms. "I won't hurt you. I'll be gentle, so gentle—"

"But—"

The word ended on a quick breath as Logan's tongue traced the sensitive line of Dawn's mouth. She shivered and unconsciously turned her head to follow the gentle, exciting caress. He smiled and nuzzled against her lips, licking the tender surface with light, sensual strokes.

"Do you like that?" he asked softly, feeling her answer in the odd, shaking breath she drew.

"Yes," she said, the word a warm sigh against his mouth. "It feels—"

The tip of his tongue flicked out, stopping her words, caressing the soft inner surface of her lips until her hand began to move slowly on his forearm.

"Do you like that, too?" he asked, his voice husky, his eyes almost gold in the firelight.

"I—"

Logan's tongue stole Dawn's mouth completely, making it his own, filling it with all the textures of a sensual man's hunger. Repeatedly he rubbed his tongue along hers in a slow, sliding caress that left her barely able to breathe. She made a tiny, wild sound in the back of her throat when he withdrew and then entered once again, swiftly, hotly. With a restraint that made his muscles like steel, he prevented himself from crushing her against the desire that was swelling fiercely between his legs. He kissed her as though her kiss were all that he could ask of her.

And in some ways it was true. At that instant he wanted nothing more than her exquisite mouth caressing him in return. As though she understood, her hands slid into his hair and her tongue tentatively stroked his. That first shy response was a pleasure so great he groaned aloud.

"Logan—? Did I do it wrong?"

"No, darling," he said thickly, nuzzling her mouth hungrily, licking her lips with tiny, restrained strokes. "You did it just right. Do it again."

There was a moment of hesitation that made Logan feel as though he were being stretched on a rack. He realized that she might have been put off by the intimacy of sharing a deep kiss.

"Never mind," he said, bringing himself under control with an effort that made him ache. "It's all right. I shouldn't ask you to—"

Dawn's mouth met Logan's with more force than finesse, effectively stopping whatever he had been going to say. After the first stunned moment of surprise, Logan gently wrested control of the kiss from her, teaching her by example how to slide her sweet tongue over his, how to stroke the secret textures of his mouth, how to nibble with exquisite care on the sensitive lower lip. He didn't teach her how to give herself to the embrace, how to invite him deeper and deeper into her warmth until he filled her mouth, how to shift and sigh and soften in his arms until he felt his heartbeat in every inch of the hardened flesh straining against his jeans. He didn't teach her those things because he didn't have to. She came to him as naturally and radiantly as dawn itself.

Logan lost himself in kissing her again and again and again. Just kissing her. He wanted more, so much more, but he was afraid she would freeze if he attempted any greater intimacy. She had acted as though she had never been kissed by a man. He had to assume that she would resist if he were to curl his hands around her breasts as he ached to do. As for undressing her and licking her nipples into hard, hungry peaks—

Logan could not stifle a small, aching groan as Dawn shifted across him in a way that pressed the softness of her breast against his biceps. Slowly his hands roamed from the black silk of her braided hair over the softness of the emerald cashmere sweater. He caressed her back, kneading lightly, letting her get used to the idea of his hands touching her. As his tongue teased her mouth his fingers teased her back. The first few times his hands moved from her spine to her ribs, Dawn stiffened at the imminent threat. Each time he retreated with a caressing, promising motion that made her shiver.

And then smoothly, slowly, inevitably, he shaped his hand to the softness of her breast.

"Logan!"

"Yes, darling?" he asked, smiling crookedly at Dawn as he bent and took her mouth once more, making an answer impossible. He didn't lift his head until her nipple had hardened and her breath was coming quickly, hotly. Satisfied, he shifted slightly away from her, removing his hand. "It will be different this time," he said, looking into her dazed green eyes.

"What?"

"You're going to watch while I touch you."

Dawn flushed to her hairline and buried her face against Logan's powerful shoulder. "I can't," she said, the words muffled against his flesh.

"Shhhh," murmured Logan, stroking her hair soothingly as he released the shining black strands from the braid's restraint. "There's no shame in being touched." His fingers moved inevitably over the emerald buttons of her cardigan. "You'll see, darling. You'll see."

Sensing how close Dawn was to fear, Logan made no attempt to strip away her sweater and bra, leaving her naked to his eyes and touch. He left her sweater partially buttoned and then eased his hand inside. For long moments he simply closed his eyes and stroked Dawn gently, enjoying the softness of cashmere against the back of his hand, and the living softness of her breast nestled against his palm. When he opened his eyes Dawn was watching him through a screen of thick black lashes.

"Go ahead," he murmured, seeing the question in her green eyes. "Ask me."

Shyly she shook her head, sending silken streamers of black hair over his hand. He smiled and carefully scraped his nails over the peak of her breast, knowing that her thin bra was no barrier to sensation. He saw the surprise and the passion that suddenly deepened the color of her eyes. Before she could recover he had flicked open the bra's fastening and enveloped her smooth flesh in his hand. He heard the tiny sound as she caught her breath. Gently he rolled her nipple between his fingertips until it was hard. He felt the sensual shivering that shook her whole body. His own breath wedged in his throat. It was all he could do not to shred the clothes from her and take her right there.

Then Logan opened his eyes and saw Dawn watching him with an expression that was divided between rising passion and fear. He bent down and kissed her quickly, wanting to tell her that it was all right, he wouldn't hurt her; but when he tried to speak his words came out as a groan of male need. With infinite care he removed his hand from her, not trusting his own control. For the first time he saw her smooth, ruby-tipped breast peeking out from between soft folds of cashmere and midnight strands of hair.

"My God," he said, his voice shaking. "You're perfect."

"Logan—"

But his name was as much a sigh of desire as it was a warning of her fear. When he bent and kissed her neck and the delicate hollow of her throat, she drew a ragged breath. Her hands moved as though to conceal her breast from his lips.

"Don't," he said huskily, looking up at her with eyes that were as passionate as his mouth. "Let me touch you the way you were meant to be touched. I don't have the words to tell you how beautiful you are. But I can show you." His eyes held hers. He sensed her hands hesitating, then falling away. "Yes," he murmured, lowering his head again. "Let me teach you how perfect you are."

At the first searing touch of his tongue on her breast, Dawn tightened like a drawn bow. Logan felt the exquisite hardening of her nipple against his tongue and wanted to shout his triumph. He drew her deeply into his mouth, consuming her with a gentle, fierce sensuality that made her shiver repeatedly. As his hand caressed her stomach and thighs he felt the deep, involuntary tightening of her body. The thought of what it would be like to be inside her and feel that passionate constriction around his hot, hard flesh made him groan. His teeth closed with sensual care on her breast. She gave a broken cry of passion and trembled against him like an aspen leaf in a summer storm.

"Logan—"

"Hold on to me, little leaf," he said, smiling gently down at her. "The storm is just beginning."

Logan turned smoothly, easily, bringing Dawn down onto the couch beside him. He didn't trap her between his body and the couch as he wanted to. Despite her passionate response, he sensed that he hadn't yet fully seduced her. Fear and desire warred equally in her eyes, in her body. He bent and licked the tips of her breasts delicately, hotly, drinking the clean scent of her even as his mouth tugged her into hard, sensual peaks.

"Logan," she moaned, twisting helplessly against him. "Oh, Logan, I shouldn't let you—" The words ended in a gasp as his hand slid between her thighs, both creating and soothing a sensual ache that transformed her. "I've never let—anyone—ah, my God!"

"I know," he said, biting her nipple with excruciating delicacy even as his hands savored the passionate heat waiting between her legs. "I know you've never let a man kiss you, undress you, taste you until you cry out. God, I know it and it's driving me crazy!" he muttered, undoing her jeans and sliding his hand inside.

For a few instants there was only the incredible silkiness of her secret flesh sliding over his fingers and the soft, wild cries he drew from her throat.

"Do you have any idea how sweet it is to know that I'm the only man who's ever touched you?" he asked hoarsely.

"No more, Logan. Please. I'm—I'm afraid," she said, pushing away from him, shivering and watching him with eyes that were almost black.

"Of me?" he asked, looking down at her, knowing she had every right to fear him. He would take everything that she had to give a man. But he would also give her what her parents no longer could, a place to live and the money to survive until she found her own niche in the world. "Don't worry, little leaf," he murmured, brushing his lips over her quivering breasts. "I'll take care of you. You can stay here while you finish school. If you want college, that's fine, too."

Then his hands and mouth ceased their soft caresses as he caught Dawn's chin, forcing her to meet his glance. His eyes were as hard as hammered gold. "But if you so much as look at another man while you're my mistress," he said softly, "I'll strip you naked and leave you penniless in the center of town."

Logan watched Dawn's luminous eyes close. A long shudder shook her body. When her eyes opened again he felt a chill move over his skin. Where passion had been there was now humiliation. Where luminous emotion had been there was—nothing. He hadn't even known that emotion had been there until he measured the echoing emptiness of its absence.

"Your mistress," she said dully.

Though Dawn didn't move, her body withdrew from his touch, leaving him empty, too.

And angry.

"What did you expect?" he snarled. "Money?"

Very slowly Dawn shook her head. The motion was enough to conceal her naked breasts beneath a midnight cloud of hair.

"Marriage and the Lazy W?"

Dawn flinched subtly, telling Logan all he needed to know. She had come here expecting to trade her virginity for the Lazy W. His frustrated desire switched instantly to pure rage as he realized that he had been nearly taken in as neatly as his dead brother Joe.

"Nice try," Logan said coldly, sitting up. "You're Mary Sue's daughter, all right. Your mother sold herself to the highest bidder—and then sold herself again whenever her gambler husband's luck was down! Well, I don't gamble anymore," Logan drawled, "so I won't be needing any wifely, uh, *services*."

Silently Dawn slid off the couch and stood up, pulling her sweater together with shaking fingers. Logan's eyes narrowed as he saw the pallor of her skin and the chills that shook her slender body.

"Just because I'm not fool enough to hand over the Lazy W doesn't mean we can't work something out," said Logan evenly. "A place for you in town, maybe."

Dawn said nothing as she walked away from him toward the staircase leading to Kathy's room.

"Sleep on it," said Logan. "It's the best offer you're going to get from any man who knew your mother. You hear?"

Dawn started climbing the steps.

"Answer me!" snarled Logan.

Slowly she turned and looked at him out of eyes that were too old to belong to a girl of eighteen. "I loved you...."

"Like hell," he said in disgust, turning away. "All you Sheridan women ever loved was the Lazy W."

Groaning, Logan rolled over, his arms flailing as though he could drive away the memories. Prowl made a disgruntled sound and resettled herself delicately next to the man's abundant heat. Logan opened his eyes and found himself staring into the cat's pale green glance. For an instant he wondered if it had been the cat's eyes haunting him through his feverish dreams and memories. Then he looked from the cat to the slender figure standing in the doorway.

"You!" he said hoarsely. "What the hell are you doing here?"

Four

Dawn stared into Logan's fierce amber eyes and felt herself go cold. He had looked at her like that three years ago when she had turned to face him before fleeing up the stairs.

I loved you.

She heard the words as clearly as though she had just spoken them. But Logan hadn't believed in her love. He had believed only in revenge. He still did.

"Ready for breakfast?" asked Dawn, her voice as carefully held as the mug steaming between her fingers.

"Breakfast!" repeated Logan. Anger climbed visibly in his pale cheeks as he threw himself to his feet. "Who the hell gave you permission to come in here like you still owned the place and—" The words stopped as abruptly as Logan himself. He swayed on the edge of unconsciousness.

"Logan!"

Heedlessly Dawn dropped the coffee mug, scalding herself even as she reached out to support him. He was unbelievably heavy. It took every bit of her strength and determination to lever him back onto the couch. He groaned as the cushions came up to meet him. His skin was cold and clammy.

"Logan," she whispered, stroking his hair as she had when he had awakened during the night. "Lie still. You're sick. The doctor will be out soon. Just lie quietly, Logan. Please."

Dawn repeated the soothing phrases many times, sensing that Logan was disoriented by his own weakness. But when his eyes opened again they were very clear, as bleak as winter. Instantly she lifted her hand from his hair and stood up, moving well beyond his reach.

"Get the hell off my ranch," said Logan.

"I will," said Dawn. "Just as soon as the doctor gives you a clean bill of health."

"Screw the doctor!" raged Logan, sitting up suddenly, then closing his eyes as the room spun again.

"Not my style," retorted Dawn swiftly. "Remember?"

Logan's eyes opened, gleaming like amber ice.

"Yes," she said in satisfaction. "I see that you do. Lie down, big man. You couldn't thumb wrestle a butterfly right now."

Logan could still swear, though, a fact that he proved very thoroughly as Dawn went to the kitchen. She returned with a bucket and a soapy rag and began wiping up the coffee she had spilled. She was grateful for the activity. It kept the tremor in her hands from showing. Even when he was too weak to stand, Logan had a sheer male presence that set every one of her nerves alight with warnings—and memories.

Logan watched the jeans stretched tightly over Dawn's hips as she scrubbed the floor. He began to swear all over again. She looked from the soapy rag to his mouth with a message that he would have to have been flat unconscious to miss. Somewhere beneath his anger, humor stirred. He slapped it down quickly.

"Try it," he invited sardonically, looking at the rag dangling from her hand.

"I never pick on people weaker than I am," she said, dropping the sloppy rag back into the bucket. "Lucky for you, huh?" she asked, turning away.

"Come back here," he demanded.

"Come and get me."

"Why you little—" Logan lunged upright and then groaned and slumped back onto the couch, missing the sudden guilty look Dawn threw over her shoulder.

"Logan?"

He opened his eyes and looked at her grimly. "Why are you here?" he asked with deceptive softness.

"I answered an ad for a zookeeper," she said. "How many eggs and what way?" she asked, walking quickly into the kitchen.

"Get off my ranch. Now."

The words were clear, implacable. Dawn was very glad that at the moment Logan was too weak to enforce the command. A searing curse broke the silence. Dawn winced and broke two eggs into boiling water. When they were done she lifted them out and put them on pieces of toasted sourdough bread. Memories from three years ago told her that Logan liked his eggs lightly salted and liberally peppered. She put silverware and a steaming coffee mug on the breakfast tray and carried it out to Logan. The look on his face was enough to make her want to run. Abruptly she decided that it was time for him to hear a few home truths.

"I called the doctor after you passed out on me last night," she said, searching Logan's hard face for signs that he was going to listen to reason. "The doctor told me that I should chain you to a bed and not let you up for at least two weeks. Four would be better. Otherwise you'll kill yourself."

"Bull," snarled Logan.

Anger swept through Dawn so suddenly and completely that she shook. She set the tray down hard on an end table and turned on Logan.

"I've got news for you, Logan Garrett—you're a man, not a machine!"

"You should know, little darling," he drawled coolly, giving her body an insolent once-over with his eyes.

Dawn felt the hot flush flooding her cheeks. "If it weren't for Kathy, I'd dump this breakfast in your lap, grab my cat and get out of this zoo."

"Kathy? What does Kathy have to do with—oh, no," gritted Logan as realization came.

"Oh *yes*," retorted Dawn. "You've got Kathy crazy with worry over you at a time when she should be worried only about herself."

"Is something wrong with her?"

"She's quite pregnant," said Dawn icily. "Or have you been so busy playing Superman that you hadn't noticed she's put on about fifty pounds?"

"Pregnancy is normal," said Logan, shrugging.

"Not when you have to fight to prevent premature birth."

"What?" asked Logan, a crack of command in his voice. "She didn't say anything to me."

"Why should she? You obviously don't give a damn about anything, including yourself." Rashly Dawn stepped forward and leaned over Logan. "Except for my grandmother, your sister is the only human being on earth who ever loved me. She never asked one thing of me in return, until two days ago. That's when I promised her that I'd take care of your house and your ranch and your stubborn carcass until the doctor said you were healthy again. So if you want to get rid of me, big man, the only way to do it is to get well.''

Logan looked at the brilliant green eyes so close to his and felt the soft weight of Dawn's long, single braid resting against his chest. His hand closed around the braid, chaining Dawn to him.

''Until I'm well,'' he said bitingly.

''Until the *doctor* says you're well,'' she amended.

He wrapped the braid around his big hand with a swiftness that shocked her. Then he released her with a motion that sent the braid flipping over her shoulder.

''My eggs are getting cold,'' he gritted, tacitly agreeing to her terms and dismissing her with the same curt sentence.

Dawn turned away, clenching her hands together so that Logan couldn't see them tremble. The depth of the emotions that had raged behind his whiskey-colored eyes had shaken her. He was a strong man and his passions ran deep. She prayed she wouldn't have to push him like that again; he had neither love nor respect for her to help bridle his anger, only his temporary physical weakness.

Aching to help, knowing that she would be curtly refused if she offered, Dawn watched Logan struggle into a sitting position. When he was ready she placed the breakfast tray across his lap and walked through the kitchen to the porch. There she folded sheets and towels and long-legged, narrow-hipped jeans until she felt enough time had passed to allow Logan to eat.

When Dawn silently walked back into the living room, Logan's eyes were closed. His face was pale, drawn, almost haggard. The sight of it went through her like a knife. For a moment she closed her own eyes, getting a grip on her emotions. She couldn't show weakness in his presence. He would sense it and use it against her now as mercilessly as he had three years ago.

Letting out her breath in a noiseless sigh, she bent over to take the tray. Her lips flattened into a grim line. Only a few bites had been taken. The rest was jumbled and smeared across the plate. Just as she opened her mouth to make a scathing comment about the quality of Logan's cooperation, she noticed the bits of egg on his shirt and the quilt and the floor. He had been too weak to feed himself and too proud to ask for help.

Fighting back the unwelcome sting of tears, Dawn cleaned up the mess and carried the tray into the kitchen. Logan ignored her, either asleep or pretending to be. A few minutes later she emerged with a new breakfast and knelt by the couch. Gently she put her hand on Logan's stubble-roughened cheek. He flinched and opened his eyes in surprise.

Without a word Dawn lifted a spoonful of cut-up eggs and toast to Logan's lips. He looked at her for a long moment before he opened his mouth. She didn't meet his eyes, afraid that her own emotions would be too clearly revealed. Breakfast was finished in silence, but he ate every bite.

"More?" she asked quietly.

"No," he said in a tight voice that told her exactly how uncertain his temper was.

"Thirsty?"

Logan nodded with a tired motion that made Dawn want to hold him, to reassure him and herself that he would be all right. Instead she took the tray back to the kitchen and returned with a glass of water. Logan held out his hand. It shook visibly. He balled his betraying fingers into a fist and let his arm drop heavily to his side. Dawn put her arm around his shoulders and held the glass to his lips as though it were the most natural thing in the world. After a single succinct curse at his own weakness, he drank from the glass until there was nothing left.

"More?" she asked softly, withdrawing her arm.

Eyes closed, Logan slumped back against the couch's support. He shook his head slowly. Without a word Dawn went to the kitchen. If she stayed she would offer him comfort, smoothing the lines of exhaustion from his forehead—and she would get her hand bitten for her trouble. Logan didn't want help or comfort from anybody. Especially from her.

A hesitant tapping from the back door cut through Dawn's thoughts. She went through the porch and opened the door. A small wiry man waited, hat in hand.

"Shorty," said Dawn, delighted to see the cowhand who had been on the Lazy W longer than she had been alive. "Come in out of the cold."

Shorty looked in disbelief at her. "Miz Sheridan? As I live and breathe—gawd damn—it is you! 'Scuse my French," he said quickly, ducking his head in embarrassment.

"I've heard a lot worse from Logan this morning," she said dryly, shutting the door behind Shorty as he walked tentatively into the glassed-in porch.

The wiry cowboy swallowed and peered around Dawn toward the kitchen. "Speak of the devil," he muttered. "He around?"

"The devil?" asked Dawn, smiling.

"Logan," muttered Shorty. "Same difference, if'n you ask me."

"He's asleep."

Shorty looked both relieved and worried. "He needs it, sure enough. But—"

"But?"

"The hands need telling what to do," said Shorty bluntly. "I been doing what I could, but I ain't no foreman and I ain't never wanted to be none."

The memory of Logan's drawn face urged Dawn to let him sleep. The knowledge that the ranch's needs couldn't be ignored made her realize that Shorty was right. She hesitated, but concern for Logan won out. A few questions brought all the information from Shorty that she needed. Quickly she told him to concentrate on preparations for moving the pregnant cows into the main pasture.

"If Logan has anything to add," she concluded, "I'll tell you later, after he wakes up."

"I'm awake now."

Dawn spun around and saw Logan leaning heavily against the kitchen door. His face was gray but his eyes burned with barely suppressed violence.

"Get this straight," he said, pinning Dawn with the deadly promise of his words. "The Lazy W belongs to a Garrett now. Bought and paid for in blood. Joe's blood. Any orders given around here get given by a Garrett, not by a Sheridan. You're not going to come out here and play grand mistress like your slut mother did. *This is my ranch, not yours.* Hear me?"

Dawn nodded, too shaken to speak.

Logan turned on Shorty. "Get those fences mended and get them done now!"

In silence Shorty and Dawn watched as Logan shoved himself away from the support of the doorframe and staggered back to the living-room couch.

"Whew," muttered Shorty after a moment. "He's well and truly pi—uh, mad." The cowboy slammed his hat on his head. "Course, he got a right to be. We all knowed that pasture fence needed mending before the cows was moved in close to home."

Gratefully Dawn accepted Shorty's delicate avoidance of the true reason for Logan's anger: he believed she wanted to take the ranch back from him.

"There should be plenty of time for the fences," she said. "The cows won't start dropping calves for nearly a month."

"Dunno," he said doubtfully. "Them range cows can be right contrary, and the Almighty knows that fence needed fixin' back before your daddy took a notion to fill an inside straight and lost the whole kit and kaboodle to Logan. It was a good deal for them cows, though. Your daddy never was worth a hoot in hell as a rancher." Shorty glanced sideways at Dawn. "Sorry, Miz Sheridan. I got no right to run off at the mouth like that. Gettin' old, I guess."

"Too old to drive into town for supplies?" asked Dawn, ignoring Shorty's reference to her father's shortcomings as a rancher. It was common knowledge in this part of Colorado that Sonny Sheridan hadn't known which end of the branding iron went in the fire.

"Sure thing," said Shorty enthusiastically. "You gonna cook for us again?"

"Who's doing it now?"

"Campbell," he said, disgust in his voice.

"Is he a new hand?" asked Dawn, not recognizing the name.

"Nope. You met him lots of times before," said Shorty, grabbing a can out of the cupboard and tossing it to her.

Dawn caught the can reflexively, looked at the label and started laughing: Campbell's pork and beans. "You poor thing," she said, returning the can to the cupboard. She handed Shorty the long supply list she had made up.

"Makes a feller drool just to look at it," said Shorty. He folded the list with reverence and tucked it into his pocket. "I'll be back in plenty of time for chow."

"Good. Otherwise Campbell rides again," she threatened.

After Shorty left, Dawn began carrying freshly washed clothes upstairs. At first she moved very carefully, afraid of calling Logan's wrath down on her head again. He seemed to be asleep—but then, she had thought he was asleep earlier. When Prowl leaped upon his chest and started kneading enthusiastically, Dawn realized that nothing short of a bucket of ice water was going to pull Logan out of his exhausted sleep. Humming quietly, she transferred his clean clothes to his closet and dresser, then swept and dusted the half of the master suite that Logan used. The other half was concealed by the sliding screen of dusty wooden panels.

Tentatively Dawn pushed the room divider aside. It slid smoothly on its tracks despite the weight of the wood itself. From the looks of the dust on the floor, no one had entered that room since the wall had been knocked out and the sliding panels put in. The furniture was covered by sheets, including what looked to be a small four-poster bed.

Suddenly something about the shape of the concealed piece of furniture tugged at Dawn. She walked swiftly to it and swept off the dustcover. Wood, polished by years of use and care, gleamed softly. Without knowing it she made a small sound and began running her hands over the smooth surfaces of her grandmother's loom. Dust, which had filtered beneath the cover, smudged her fingers. She didn't notice. She sat on the bench, positioned her feet on the harness pedals and worked each of them in turn. Segments of the loom shifted smoothly and returned to position, picking up imaginary threads of the warp, making room for the shuttle to pass through and then closing up again.

The sounds of the old loom were as familiar as the beat of her own blood in her veins. She had spent thousands of hours in this room, watching and learning from her grandmother, feeling the magic of separate threads uniting into a whole that was both beautiful and unexpected. It was to this room she had come when she wanted reassurance and love, excitement and serenity, continuity and hope. To her the gleaming loom was a piece of magic as extraordinary as any enchanted castle or winged horse. It called to her as nothing had but Logan, the man she had loved even before she knew she was capable of love.

But Logan saw her only as Mary Sue's daughter, wanting only the ranch, not the man. He never saw Dawn as a woman capable of love. A woman who loved him.

After a long, long time, Dawn looked up from her memories and dreams, hopes and regrets. The bare, dirty, glaring squares of the windows stared back at her.

You couldn't change the past, could you, magic loom? she thought, stroking the smooth wood. *You couldn't change the warp and weft of those sad, wasted lives. I can't change them, either. I can only try to gather the tangled ends and begin to weave again.*

Dawn's eye was caught by a flash of blue as a car drove up to the ranch house and stopped. A very solidly built man got out, carrying a medical bag in one ham-sized fist. Dawn touched the loom a final time before she got up and hurried downstairs to let the doctor in.

"Miss Sheridan?" asked the man as she opened the door.

"Dawn," she said, holding out her hand.

"Dr. Martin," he said, shaking her hand and shouldering past her into the living room in the same motion. "How's our prize fool doing?"

"Er, Logan?" she asked, closing the door against the brash March wind.

"Know any other prize fools?" asked the doctor, his black eyes gleaming.

"I'm afraid so," she murmured, thinking of herself, "but he's the only prize fool who needs a doctor at the moment."

Dr. Martin grunted and headed for the couch where Logan was sprawled. The doctor took Logan's pulse and blood pressure, listened to his lungs and heart, muttered, felt the heat of Logan's skin and shook him awake with more efficiency than gentleness. As soon as the amber eyes focused on him, the doctor began speaking.

"You're a damn fool, Logan Garrett!"

"Hello, Doc," said Logan, smiling slightly. "Did Shorty call you out here to check on that lame mare?"

"I should be so lucky," retorted Dr. Martin. "A vet's patients get the medicine shoved down their throats or up their arses and they either get better or die. They don't refuse to take pills and then lie around mouthing off to their doctor."

"That's why they call them dumb animals," retorted Logan, but his voice was weak.

Dr. Martin grabbed Logan's wrist and took the pulse again. "You're pretty done, boy. Just talking makes your heartbeat pick up. You believe me yet?"

"Yeah," said Logan, his voice rich with disgust. "I believe you."

"Going to stay in bed this time?"

A mutinous look settled on Logan's hard features.

"Yes," said Dawn firmly, "he'll stay in bed."

"You sure?" asked Dr. Martin, measuring Logan's expression.

"I'm sure," she said. "He can't get rid of me until you give him a clean bill of health."

"That," said Dr. Martin dryly, looking at Dawn's slender feminine grace, "does *not* reassure me."

"Have you lived here long?" asked Dawn.

"Two years. I retired out of Steamboat Springs and then got bored. When the old doctor broke his hip, I took over."

Dawn nodded. "Have you heard the story of Joe Garrett and Mary Sue Sheridan yet?"

Dr. Martin looked uneasily at Logan, whose face was utterly without expression. "No more than a hundred times," said the doctor dryly. "Why?"

"I'm Mary Sue's daughter." Dawn saw the doctor's wind-reddened face change expression. "Logan will do whatever he has to in order to get rid of me," she continued, "including lie flat on his back until he's well."

Dr. Martin looked from his patient to the pale, beautiful woman whose eyes were the color of spring. He sighed and began giving Dawn instructions on the care and feeding of a prize fool. When he was finished he pulled a lethal looking hypodermic out of his case.

"Just as well you aren't going riding for a while," said Dr. Martin.

"Out," said Logan to Dawn.

She turned on her heel and left without argument.

"Coffee?" the doctor called hopefully after her as he peeled down Logan's jeans and swabbed off a segment of his muscular buttocks.

"Cream and sugar?" asked Dawn from the kitchen.

"Is it Logan's kind of coffee?" retorted Dr. Martin, sliding the needle in with smooth skill.

Logan began swearing beneath his breath.

"It's ranch coffee," she admitted.

"Cream and sugar, then. Lots." Dr. Martin withdrew the needle, slapped a circular bandage on the spot and hiked Logan's jeans back into place. "Such language, boy," he said, then spoiled it by laughing. He began poking and prodding Logan's body. "When was the last time you used the bathroom?"

"Last night," said Logan grudgingly.

"Uh-huh. Think you can make it to the john or do you want a pan?"

What Logan thought wasn't suitable for conversation—even with a doctor.

"Okay, cowboy," said Dr. Martin. "Let's get you up those stairs. You'll be better off in a real bed."

With Dr. Martin's help Logan climbed the stairs. The bathroom he managed by himself. Then he fell into bed feeling as though he had just spent twenty hours branding steers. He was asleep within seconds.

Dr. Martin listened to Logan's breathing for several minutes before he went back downstairs to where Dawn waited.

"Is he—all right?" asked Dawn, her voice strained to the point of breaking.

"He's better than he has any right to be," grunted the doctor. "Never saw a stronger man in my life. Given half a chance, his body will heal. He hasn't given it half a chance, though. He didn't believe me when I told him he had walking pneumonia." The doctor took a swig of creamy coffee. "Now he's got three choices. Bed, hospital or hell."

Dawn flinched.

"Somehow," continued Dr. Martin, "you've talked him out of the last one. If you can keep him in bed for three weeks—even two weeks, given his constitution—he'll be on his way." The doctor hesitated then looked Dawn straight in the eye. "You listen to his breathing real close, honey. If it changes, don't bother to call me. Just get Logan in a car and bring him to the hospital."

"Should he be there now?" she asked tightly.

"If he'll stay in bed, he's better off here. Less chance of catching an infection." Dr. Martin drained the mug and put it back on the counter with a soft thump. "I'll be out again tomorrow."

As Dr. Martin's car pulled out of the ranch yard, Dawn stood next to Logan's bed, her fingertips resting lightly on his wrist, trying to count his heartbeats. Her own racing heart interfered. There were no chairs in the room, and she was too tired to stand any longer. She lay down carefully on the far side of the bed, her arm stretched full length so that she could touch Logan's wrist. It was hot, too hot, but her fingertips sensed the strong pulse of his life. His breathing was the same, both rhythmic and deep.

After a long time Dawn slept, reassured by the feel of Logan's heart beating beneath her fingertips.

Five

The muted sound of the old four-harness loom filled the room where Logan slept. Dawn had opened the room divider so that she could watch him while she worked. The room itself was as clean as the clothes she had folded and put in Logan's dresser. The windows and loom had been polished until they gleamed. Bright yarns bloomed like unexpected flowers in every corner of the room. The shuttle flew in Dawn's hands, weaving a muted shimmer of bronze yarn into a very loose gauze pattern, using techniques that had been ancient when men built their cities of clay. Beside her a kitchen timer ticked softly, ready to remind her when it was time to turn bread out of warm metal pans. A rich aroma of fresh bread permeated the house.

Slowly Logan opened his eyes, feeling fully conscious for the first time since he had staggered into the living room and fallen across the couch. He had slept for most of the first four days Dawn had been there, waking only to be fed or to

wobble into the bathroom. Then for the next two weeks he
had done little more except rest and absorb the soothing
rhythms of Dawn's loom, his aggressive will chained by the
fever medicine-sedative that Dr. Martin had prescribed
along with the antibiotics. Beneath the passivity enforced by
the medicine, Logan's body had healed itself quickly, gaining strength with each hour. He had watched the process as
though at a distance, measuring his increasing strength by
the ease with which he moved from bed to bathroom and
back, vaguely wondering at his own lack of protest.

Today was different. Today he hadn't been given the
medicine. He had awakened feeling eager, alert, alive, as
though the world had come into focus while he slept.

He turned his head toward the loom whose sounds had
woven in and out of his healing sleep. As he watched, the
vertical lines of yarn on the loom shifted in rhythmic se-
quence, fascinating him. The motions of the loom and
Dawn's graceful throwing of the shuttle from side to side as
she wove were like the sound of the loom itself—subtly re-
laxing, almost serene. Each time Dawn worked the harness
pedals, the black silk of her unbound hair shifted, weaving
light into new patterns as surely as she was creating new
fabric on the loom.

Braided. Her hair should be braided, thought Logan idly.

His right hand closed on itself as he remembered how it
had felt to hold the cool satin weight of the braid in his
palm. He also remembered the sliding caress of the braid
over his chest when Dawn bent down to touch his forehead.

Without breaking the motion of her work, Dawn hung the
shuttle on the loom's frame and picked up another shuttle
that held a slightly different shade of bronze yarn. Deftly she
wove the new color into the old, shifted her feet on the harness pedals and threw the shuttle through the new opening
she had just created.

The swift progress of the weaving amazed Logan. *Magic.* Then, almost helplessly, a question came: *How can a man stand against that kind of magic?*

The echo of his own thoughts angered him. The long days of watching her while he drifted in and out of fevered dreams must have softened his brain. Dawn wasn't magic, and he wasn't enough of a fool to forget Joe's example. Joe had believed that there was only one woman for·him. When he couldn't have her, he had turned his rage at life on himself, blaming himself for Mary Sue's fickle nature. Logan's mouth thinned as the familiar anger stirred deep within his mind. He wouldn't make Joe's mistake. He wouldn't let a woman turn him inside out so she could watch him bleed to death.

For the first time in weeks Logan felt strong enough to fight back.

"What do you think you're doing?" he asked, his voice hard.

Startled, Dawn turned swiftly toward Logan. "Weaving." She looked intently at him, registering the alertness of his eyes and the healthy color of his skin. "How do you feel?"

"I can see that," he retorted, ignoring her question about his health. "What are you weaving?"

"Curtains," she said, glancing automatically at the bedroom windows where light came like a blow through the unshielded glass.

"I don't need any," he said flatly.

"*You* don't," agreed Dawn. "The windows do."

"No," he said coldly. "I hate windows that are all tarted up and covered over like a cathouse párlor."

Dawn stopped weaving. She stood, went to a card table she had set up near her loom and picked up what looked like a handful of bronze smoke. The weaving was very open, almost nonexistent. Without speaking she threaded a slender

wooden rod through a hem in the loose fabric. When she
was finished she shook the rod. Darkly gleaming threads
settled into an asymmetrical, pleasing pattern of loops and
gauzy weave. She went to the window by Logan's bed, stood
on tiptoe and eased the rod over the two hooks that waited
to receive it. Immediately the light coming through the
window gentled into a shimmering richness of pale gold.

Logan sat up with an ease that startled Dawn. He looked
out of the window. The fragile weaving didn't interfere with
his view of the Rockies shouldering a cloud-swept, sun-
washed sky. He grunted noncommittally and returned his
attention to her. Dawn waited for a moment, then went back
across the room. Logan's amber eyes watched the swaying,
hip-length curtain of her hair as she walked to the loom.

When Dawn leaned forward to pick up the shuttle,
strands of midnight hair slid forward. Logan found himself holding his breath for fear that some of the black silk
would become painfully tangled within the weaving.

"Watch it," he said huskily. "You're going to end up part
of the curtains."

She gave him a swift sideways look and a hesitant smile.
Her slender fingers combed through the thickness of hair
falling to her hips, checking to see how damp the strands still
were from being washed. "Almost dry. By the time the
bread is done I'll be able to braid it."

"The bread?" asked Logan with a whimsy that surprised him almost as much as it did her.

"That's a thought. Have you ever had braided lemon
bread?" asked Dawn, tossing her hair back over her shoulder with an automatic gesture.

"No. Sounds good," he said absently, watching as Dawn
worked with what looked like a thick, soft bronze string. His
amber eyes followed her intently. After a few minutes he still
couldn't figure out the mechanics of weaving. Her hands
and feet moved so swiftly on the loom that his eye couldn't

follow. "How do you do that?" he asked rather plaintively.

A silky curtain of midnight hair hid Dawn's small smile.
That was exactly the same question she had asked her
grandmother years and years ago.

"See the tight vertical strands of yarn above where I'm
weaving?" asked Dawn. "That's called the warp."

"Looks like string to me."

"In weaving, everything is called yarn, even when it looks
more like string or thread," explained Dawn.

Logan grunted. "Warp. What's that thing in your hand?"

"A shuttle. It carries yarn through the warp. The opening that the shuttle moves through between the strands of
warp," she continued, "is called the shed. When you weave,
the shuttle takes yarn through the shed. The new row of yarn
laid down by the shuttle becomes part of the weft, which is
always woven at a right angle to the warp. In most kinds of
weaving the warp determines the design, so if it isn't laid
down correctly in the beginning, the cloth will be a mess."

Dawn slowed her work and demonstrated how to weave
at about one-tenth her normal speed. All of the warp yarns
were at the moment perfectly parallel. Her foot came down
on the first harness pedal. Logan narrowed his eyes as he
watched the warp yarns being shifted out of parallel by the
harness, rather like an archer's hand drawing a bowstring.
Some warp yarns were pulled down, others were pulled up.
The shuttle moved through the opening, or shed, in a single
swoop, laying down the weft. Her foot shifted, releasing one
harness and bringing another into play. Warp yarns shifted
as well. Instead of every other yarn being pulled up, every
third yarn was. Others were pulled down. The shuttle moved
through the new shed, laying down a new row of weft.
Shifting her weight, Dawn brought the first and third harnesses into use, creating an entirely new shed—and weft
pattern.

"Most of the time I use a comb or a weaver's sword to pack the weft into place before I weave another row. The harder I pack and the closer together the warp yarns are laid, the more dense the weave. But I wanted these curtains to be nothing more than a gentle filter, so I laid the warp yarns at least a half-inch apart. Same for the weft."

While Dawn spoke her weaving speed automatically picked up until the loom murmured rhythmically again as harness pedals worked and the warp shifted into new alignments. Logan watched, even more fascinated now that he knew how the weaving was accomplished. Dawn made what he sensed was a very complicated process look as natural as breathing.

And to her it was.

"I thought weavings were all plaid," said Logan after a time.

Dawn's laugh was as gentle as the light shimmering through the newly curtained window. "Plaid is a common pattern because it's so inevitable in weaving. The design colors come together at right angles, just like the warp and the weft itself."

"You don't like plaids," said Logan. It wasn't a question. Somehow he knew that Dawn and plaids weren't a natural combination.

"Some of them are very complex, very beautiful," she said. As she spoke she changed shuttles for one that held a slightly more golden shade of bronze. With a few twisting, graceful moments she tied off the old weft yarn and wove in the new.

"But?" prodded Logan, wanting to pry beneath the surface of the woman who was so maddeningly serene.

"But plaids are too...predictable," she admitted. "Nongeometric designs are more difficult, much harder to control and much more rewarding for me to weave."

"You're too good for plain old plaids, is that it?" he taunted.

"Just like you," she retorted.

"What?"

"I washed every shirt in your closet. Not one of them was plaid."

There was a long silence. Dawn looked over at Logan. His eyes were closed and he was very still. She let out a silent breath of relief. Without the fever medicine to blunt Logan's temper, he was rapidly turning back into his usual rough-edged self. She knew that the better he felt, the harder he would be on her. It was difficult enough for him to appear weak before anyone. To be weak in front of Mary Sue's daughter was insufferable for a man of Logan's anger and pride. But he had to suffer it until he was fully recovered.

Dawn had no doubt that Logan wouldn't suffer alone.

The timer buzzed softly at her elbow then subsided. She stood, stretched with unconscious grace and faced the bed. "Need anything from the kitchen?"

Logan started to refuse curtly, then realized that he was hungry. "Is it lunchtime?" he asked grudgingly.

"Whenever you're hungry it's time to eat. I'm a weaver, not a seamstress. I don't want to spend the next five weeks taking in your shirts."

"You don't have to spend the next five weeks doing a damn thing for me!" he shot back quickly. "Anytime you want to shag your butt out my front door it's fine with me."

"Umm," she agreed, giving him a sassy grin despite the hurt she couldn't help feeling. *Don't be a fool, Dawn,* she scolded herself. *You can't give him anything more to use against you than he already has.* "All you have to do is get well, big man, and I'll be out that door like a shot out of a rifle."

Logan watched Dawn's hair swirl in a silky cloud as she spun toward the bedroom door. He thought of what it had felt like three years ago when that cool silk had fanned across his hand and her breast, concealing both. An impossible hunger tightened his loins. When he felt the heavy hot ache spreading throughout his body he made a sound of disgust and rolled over onto his stomach. He was supposed to be too weak to walk to the barn and yet he got hard just at the thought of touching Dawn. If it was this bad now, it would be pure hell in the next few weeks.

Is that how Joe felt every time he thought of Mary Sue?

The thought was like being dropped into ice water. Chills swept through Logan's body, driving out passion and need, leaving only an anger as frigid as winter itself.

Dawn sensed the difference as soon as she stepped into the room. After the subtle camaraderie they had enjoyed while he watched her weave, the icy contempt on his face as he looked at her was like a slap. She set a pitcher of milk and a plate of warm, honeyed bread on the bedside table and returned to her loom. As she walked, her hands flew through her hair, braiding it. She tied a snippet of yarn around the end of the braid, flipped it over her shoulder and picked up the shuttle once more.

Logan ate the food she had brought to him, watched her weave with brooding amber eyes and slept fitfully, more bored than tired. When he awoke again the empty plate had been removed. A fragrant bowl of soup steamed gently on the tray. He knew that the soup would taste even better than it smelled and that every ingredient in it would be as fresh as the April sunlight spilling into the bedroom. Next to the soup were slices of bread that were still warm from the oven.

Hungrily he reached for the food, both enjoying and resenting the fact that Dawn had gone to all this trouble for him.

Not for me. For Kathy. Dawn doesn't even know that I gave her that money.

The thought sent a peculiar feeling through Logan, an emotion as ambivalent as his reaction to the fresh food she had prepared. On the one hand it would give him a fierce satisfaction if Dawn knew that she was in his debt. On the other hand he didn't want to answer any questions about why he had given her the money in the first place.

And it had been a gift, not a loan. He hadn't expected one damn thing in return. Certainly not this, a tray with home-made bread and a warm, damp cloth that smelled of fresh lemon.

Logan shook out the cloth and buried his face in it, in-haling deeply. He didn't ask himself how Dawn had known that he was feeling stale and gritty even though he had done nothing but lie in bed. He didn't wonder how she had known that the crisp citrus scent revived him the way a summer rain revived a pine forest.

She did it to please me.

And the next, darker thought: *She wants to get her hooks into me as deeply as Mary Sue did into Joe.*

But did Mary Sue do anything this gentle for Joe? Ever? Even once in her selfish life?

The question had no answer. When Joe had gotten drunk and talked about Mary Sue, it wasn't her gentleness that had consumed him. It was her dark hair and high breasts and the silky motion of her hips as she walked.

Like Dawn. Silk in motion.

Logan threw down the washrag and began to eat. From across the room Dawn glanced once at his angry face, then turned her attention to the gauzy curtain she was weaving. She didn't expect Logan to thank her for taking care of him, but it disturbed her that everything she did seemed to make him harder, harsher, more angry. She did so little, too. Food, clean bedding, conversation when he permitted it.

So little . . .

Blindly Dawn threw the shuttle through the sheds the harnesses created. It wasn't the warp and weft that she saw with her clear green eyes. It was memories of Logan stretched out on the bed wearing the snug cotton briefs that were all he would tolerate as pajamas. Even ill, feverish and surly, he called to her senses as nothing ever had. Each time she touched him, each time she felt his supple, powerful body beneath her hands, she remembered how it had felt to tremble in his arms. The memories were like a hot sweet wine stealing through her, melting her inhibitions and fears. She couldn't help wondering what it would have been like if Logan had continued touching her so intimately three years ago, making her cry out her hunger and her need and her love until he joined his body to hers.

No!

The frantic thought ripped through Dawn's control. The shuttle jerked and nearly dropped from her fingers. With a quick motion she recovered the rhythm of her weaving.

Don't think about making love with Logan. And don't call it by coy little euphemisms like "making love." It's sex, pure and simple. It's what happened to Mary Sue. She couldn't control herself so she ended up destroying everything she touched. I won't be like her. I won't! I won't leave a tangle of wasted lives behind me.

But you love Logan, and you know he wants you, whispered another part of Dawn's mind. *Couldn't love lay down a straight, clean warp and create a beautiful, passionate weaving?*

Dawn had no answer unless it was in her own hands, hungry to touch Logan.

The sound of Logan's spoon clattering against the tray drew Dawn out of her disturbing reverie. She looked over. Logan's color was normal. His eyes were clear and his hands were no longer weak. He sat up easily, his bare shoulders dark against the pale sheet. Each time he breathed, each

time he moved, the vitality that had returned to him reached
out to her senses as surely as the sunlight flooding the room.
She wanted to go to him, to sit by his side and talk about the
past that was tearing both of them apart, about Joe's life
and death and Mary Sue's futile sensuality.

But even the thought of stirring Logan's anger and her
own hunger for his love frightened Dawn. It was too soon.
Logan still wanted revenge. The further away he got from
sickness, the clearer his anger became. Too soon. Perhaps
it would always be too soon. Perhaps the bleak, ugly pattern of Joe Garrett and Mary Sue Sheridan had no end.

The shuttle flew from side to side, independent of Dawn's
thoughts as she searched for a hopeful pattern among the
tangled skeins of past and present lives. Beneath her flying
fingers another airy weaving grew, a gentle design for cap-
turing and caressing the raw power of sunlight before letting it flow through her net unharmed. It was what she
would do for Logan if she could—take the raw force of his
anger and let it pass through the golden weaving of her love,
filtering out the destruction, allowing the vital radiance of
him to shine through.

But how could she filter out his lifelong hunger for revenge? Did he even know how destructive his search for
vengeance had become?

"There's a good wet snowpack in the high country," said
Dawn, glancing quickly at Logan before continuing her
weaving. "The grass should hold all summer."

Logan turned and looked out the bedroom window for a
moment. The snow-laden mountain peaks were hidden by a
wild tumble of clouds through which poured shafts of
flashing sunlight, but he didn't need to see the mountains to
know what was happening. As the ground and the snowpack slowly thawed, water would begin to move both on the
surface and beneath the earth. It was the hidden ground-
water that nourished the grasses that his cattle depended

upon. Without that slow, invisible movement of meltwater beneath the soil, the grass would head out and dry up too soon, forcing him to resort to expensive supplemental feeding of his cows long before autumn snows closed off the high pastures.

"Yeah," said Logan, settling back against the pillows. "Should be a good year. Unless something goes wrong."

"Like a spring blizzard?"

Logan grunted. "Shorty better get those fences fixed or I'll have his hide for a saddle blanket. If the cows start to drift south in front of a blizzard, we'll have hell's own time saving the calves in that broken country beyond the big pasture."

The loom murmured rhythmically, drawing his eyes toward the gleaming wood. Dawn's profile was like the sunlight pouring into the bedroom—both serene and infused with a vibrant energy.

"Granddad used to dread spring," said Dawn. "The cows would drift in front of the wind until they were way up into Pine Chute and Gray Rock and Avalanche Creek. Then they'd calve in snow up to their hocks even though the lower valleys had been swept clean by the wind and the sun. Lord, how he used to cuss those cows for contrariness."

From the corner of her eye she saw Logan smile crookedly. She knew that he had liked her grandfather, a man who said hello before he counted the number of acres or cows a man owned. Nate Sheridan had been as blunt and unpretentious as a granite boulder. So unlike Sonny, who had been very impressed with his family's wealth and his own position as the son of the richest rancher for a hundred miles in any direction. Sonny had been sure that money made him better than other men. He had lorded it over everyone, especially Joe Garrett, whose easygoing generosity and rugged good looks had made him a favorite among his peers of both sexes.

"Is that why your granddad put double fences across the mouths of those little valleys?" asked Logan, frowning as he remembered the state of disrepair of those same fences. He had assumed that they were meant to protect the valleys from summer grazing, not from cows drifting in front of winter storms. He'd have to speak to Shorty about repairing those as well as the big pasture fence.

"Yes," said Dawn, throwing the shuttle gracefully through the opening the harnesses had just created. "Grandpa swore that he had lost his last calf to high-country snowbanks."

"Had he?"

Dawn gave Logan a sidelong, pitying glance. "That fever must have affected your brain. Anyone who raises cows in this part of Colorado loses some calves in the snow."

Logan watched the shadow that crossed Dawn's face even as she spoke. "Feeling sorry for your granddad? Don't. He knew the risks."

"I'm feeling sorry for the calves," admitted Dawn. "They don't have any choices to make. Snow or grass, blizzard or warm sun, calves get born. And some of them die before they even get a chance to stand up and drink the warm milk that's waiting for them. It always seemed to cruel to me."

Silently Logan measured the clouds gathering around the snowy peaks, but he was seeing as well the calves he had dug out of snowstorms and slung over his saddle, fighting his way back to the barn's life-saving warmth. It was brutal work for both man and horse. Yet there were few things in life as rewarding as bringing to life a calf that had been all but dead in the snow, watching it stir and suck lustily on a man's fingers, looking for the milk that it instinctively knew had to be somewhere close.

"You can save some of them," said Logan softly.

Dawn saw the gentleness of his expression and felt a strange frisson of warmth shiver through her. She remem-

bered what Kathy had said about Logan's responses to the
twins, how much he loved them, how good he was with
them. Surely a man who was that gentle with helpless creatures could also be gentle with a woman who wanted nothing more than to see him healed in spirit as well as in body?

"Yes," she murmured. "That's what makes the pain and
the frustration and the anger over losing calves all worth it—
watching a calf that you saved frolic in a spring meadow."

Logan saw the flash of Dawn's smile and the elegant sensuality of her movements as she wove. Suddenly he wanted
to hold her, to pull her feminine warmth around him, to
have her always smile at him as though he were sunrise after
a long time of night. Yet when he heard his own thoughts,
uneasiness and anger rippled through him. He might want
her, but he sure as hell didn't *need* her in any but a temporary, purely sexual way. Her warmth was an illusion. So was
her gentleness. So was the radiance that at times made her
shimmer with life.

Illusion. All of it. She was a user and a destroyer. It could
be no other way with Mary Sue's daughter.

"Of course," he said sardonically, "the calf you saved
grows up and is killed for beef."

The loom beat rhythmically, a giant heart marking time
in the suddenly silent room.

"Every living thing dies," said Dawn finally, wondering
what she had said to make Logan turn on her. "Is that any
reason not to enjoy and enhance the life around us?"

"Is that what your mother was doing? Enhancing the life
of everything in pants?"

The giant heartbeat faltered for an instant, then resumed
as Dawn wove a fragile web of gold in which to gentle the
raw power of the sun.

"You'll have to ask the men if they were enhanced," she
said quietly.

"I'd be dead before I could talk to half of them," retorted Logan.

"But then, you don't really have to talk to them at all," said Dawn. "You already know, don't you?"

"Damn right I do."

"Because of Joe?"

There was a long, tight silence that made Dawn regret bringing up Joe's name. Yet the past had to be talked about if there were to be any hope for a more constructive future. Better to talk now while illness dulled Logan's strength and temper. Later he would be too strong, too self-controlled to tolerate new answers to old questions.

"Tell me about Joe," said Dawn, weaving smoothly, gracefully, wanting to look at Logan and very much afraid of doing so. "All I know is what I've overheard at round-ups and poker games."

There was another time of silence. She glanced quickly at Logan. His expression was angry now, almost brutal. She took a deep breath and reminded herself that this was necessary. It was the only way to break the pattern of silence and rage and revenge that had become Logan's life.

"What did you hear about Joe?" demanded Logan harshly.

Frantically Dawn searched among her memories for ones that wouldn't set a match to Logan's explosive temper. "I heard that he was very good-looking in a rugged sort of way. Like the mountains," she said. Her voice was low, musical, as though she were trying to soothe a cornered animal. "Big, strong, easygoing, always ready to have a good time, a hard worker, a better judge of cattle than of—" Abruptly she stopped talking.

"Women?" offered Logan softly. Too softly.

"That goes without saying, doesn't it? He was a good rancher when he wasn't—" Again Dawn curbed her memories before she pointed out that Joe had been a notorious drunk as well as a rotten judge of women.

"You must have spent a lot of time at your mother's knee," Logan said coolly, "listening to her tell lies about the man she ruined."

Dawn turned and faced Logan in the silent room, feeling suddenly cornered herself, angry, forced to confront memories of her own that she liked no better than Logan liked his. Maybe if he knew that her own life had been less than happy, maybe then he could forgive her for being born to the wrong mother.

"Time at Mary Sue's knee?" repeated Dawn, her voice no longer musical. "Not likely, Logan. And that's how I think of her. Mary Sue, not Mother. Grandmother was my true mother. Mary Sue just happened to be the one who got pregnant with me." Dawn searched Logan's face but saw no softening of his hostility toward her. She turned back to the loom and the rhythmic beat resumed. "As for Mary Sue lying about Joe, I never heard her mention your brother."

Logan thought of all the nights of his childhood when he had listened to Joe ramble on about Mary Sue, about her stunning beauty and her brutal coldness, about her sexy smile and her cruel laughter, about the lust she could raise in a man, leaving him too weak too move. The knowledge that Mary Sue had never even thought about the man she ruined enraged Logan more than any insults she could have passed on to Dawn.

"That doesn't bother you, does it?" he asked in a soft, dangerous voice.

"What?"

"That you're the daughter of a woman who ruined a good man and never even regretted it for a moment. You're as cold a bitch as she is."

Logan saw the change in Dawn's expression; color bleached from her cheeks. It gave him a black, savage satisfaction that Mary Sue might have been invulnerable where the Garrett men were concerned, but Dawn wasn't. She could be hurt. Like Joe had been hurt.

"You know less about me than I know about Joe," said Dawn, her voice shaking. "Yet you've always been ready to believe the worst of me. Why?"

The stark question made Logan uncomfortable for an instant, but only for an instant. "Look in the mirror. Like mother like daughter. Well, I've got a bulletin for you. I'm not as nice as Joe was about being teased. You get me hard and you pay the price."

Dawn looked over at Logan. She closed her eyes and felt ice moving in her veins. There was no mercy in him; he meant every word. "I don't have any control over your body," she said almost desperately.

His laugh was no softer than the flat line of his mouth. "No control? God, I wish Joe were still alive. He'd die laughing instead of crying for Mary Sue."

"Logan, I've never done anything to tease you or any man," said Dawn urgently, knowing that somehow she had to make him understand that she wasn't her mother. "Look at me! I don't wear makeup or tight clothes or—"

"You were born cold," interrupted Logan harshly, "but your body makes men burn. They ache for you, and you turn and walk away without caring."

"That's not true!"

"The hell it isn't. Or did you think you were doing me a favor three years ago when you left me hurting for you?"

"If I had stayed, you would have made me into exactly what my mother was. A tramp. I needed love, Logan, not—"

"Sex?" finished Logan smoothly. "Too bad. Sex I've got a lot of. But love? No way. Like I said, I'm not as nice as Joe. And even if I was, I'd have to be a pure damn fool to show it to a whore's daughter."

Silently Logan watched Dawn get up and leave the bedroom, wishing he could take more satisfaction in having been the one to remove the color from her cheeks. But there was only disgust, not pleasure.

After a long time he slept fitfully, dreaming that he was naked in a blizzard, dying of cold, calling Dawn's name.

And hearing Mary Sue's laughter in return.

Six

Dawn carried away Logan's dinner tray and went downstairs with eager strides, wanting to be through in the kitchen and back upstairs with Logan. She looked forward to the evenings with him, despite the fact that like Colorado's uneven spring he could turn cold and cutting without any warning. And, like spring, he could be so warm and gentle that he made her heart turn inside out with a convulsive surge of life and hope.

Silly little leaf, she said to herself. *Logan doesn't care about my hope or my hurt. He's only decent to me when I avoid the subject of the past. And the longer I avoid the past the more I hope and the more I hurt when Joe's ghost rises again.*

Yet she couldn't help hoping. Each one of Logan's rare smiles became a memory that melted her. Each time she touched him, no matter how impersonally, she felt awareness spread through her in a shivering wave of heat.

He thinks I'm cold. Then on the heels of that thought came an icy hail of reality. *God help me if Logan finds out how I really feel. It's too soon. He still wants vengeance, not love.*

And each day I love him more.

Seeing him tangled in the past was like seeing a magnificent wild stallion tangled in a barbed-wire fence. With each surge of strength, each thoughtless upheaval of power, the cruel wire wrapped tighter, dug in deeper; and so the stallion struggled harder, increasing the destructive tangle until he gave up in exhaustion and bled to death.

Or until someone came and cut the wires, freeing him. Someone who knew that her thanks were likely to consist of a savaging such as few people survived. Someone who was as helplessly drawn into the elemental tangle as the stallion itself. Someone who prayed that if she were very gentle, if she talked soothingly and touched him with loving care, maybe then he wouldn't cut her to ribbons as soon as he was on his feet again. Maybe. But even if there was only a small chance of success, she had to try. She couldn't live with herself knowing that she had walked away from pain that she might have been able to ease.

You're a fool, Dawn Sheridan. Who's going to ease your pain?

There was no answer. There never had been, after her grandmother had died. Except for Kathy and the big man who was Kathy's brother, the man who had once healed Dawn's fear of men with his caresses—only to wound her as no one ever had before or since.

"Dawn?"

Logan's voice came easily down the stairs and into the kitchen where Dawn was putting odds and ends into the dishwasher.

"Coming," she called. "Do you need something?"

"Don't suppose you have any pie hidden away down there?" he asked hopefully.

"I was going to surprise you."

"Not likely," he retorted, his drawl emphasized by the laughter he was trying to conceal. "I've been smelling cherry pie since before dinner, and that was hours ago."

"Thank God you can't smell ice cream," muttered Dawn, thinking of the other half of her surprise— homemade ice cream.

"What?" called Logan.

"Nothing. I'll be up in a minute."

She went to the freezer and got out a small shiny bucket of French vanilla ice cream. By the time she got another tray ready she could hear Logan pacing around the room. She wanted to yell at him to go back to bed, but she didn't. She knew that he was at that awkward stage of recuperation—not well enough to be on his feet all the time, and far too well to take kindly to lying around. Besides, if she told him to go back to bed, they would argue, and they hadn't argued all day. It would be a shame to spoil that record when bedtime was only a few hours off.

Dawn was careful to make an unusual amount of noise on the stairway and to walk slowly enough to give Logan time to be back in bed when she opened the door. The latter was not only to avoid an argument, but to save herself the fascination and shock of seeing him nude. Once Logan had gotten well enough to dress himself, he had refused to wear clothes of any kind in bed. It was a subject Dawn didn't feel comfortable arguing about, because since he had learned that he could make her blush with his maleness or his teasing innuendos, he brought color to her cheeks at every opportunity.

Logan watched Dawn come into the bedroom with the big tray in her arms. He didn't know which looked better—the cherry pie with its softly melting mounds of ice cream or the cherry-red lips and creamy skin of the woman who was bringing dessert to him. It occurred to him for the hundredth time that he would like to take her to bed like an all-day sucker.

Yet he knew if he said anything like that to Dawn she would retreat. Whatever her experiences with men after she had run from him, they hadn't been good. Maybe she'd learned the hard way not to tease men. Maybe one or more of them had held her down and made her deliver on every one of the promises that husky voice and sexy body made.

The idea should have pleased Logan, but it didn't. The thought of some stranger punishing Dawn enraged Logan. Deep inside he felt that she was his to punish or soothe, his to enjoy or destroy, his to take to bed or to ignore. He would be the only male evening up the score between the Garrett men and the Sheridan women.

And there were better ways than rape to even that score. Much better. Dawn was vulnerable to him physically. He knew it as surely as he knew that her hands trembled and her breath caught when she brushed against him. If he could be patient for a while longer, she would get hungry enough to forget her caution and come softly to him, offering herself. At that moment he would have her in the palm of his hand.

Then he would close it, crushing her, evening the score forever.

After that, when ranchers gathered around in front of the store or the church to talk, it wouldn't be about crazy Joe Garrett who had drunk himself to death over a tramp—it would be about the tramp's daughter, who had fallen into the same sensual trap her mother had set for Joe.

All it would take was time and the right bait. Logan knew he had plenty of both.

Logan smiled up at Dawn, knowing from the way her eyes widened and her mouth softened in response that she liked his smiles. "Looks good enough to eat," he said, his voice almost rough.

"That's what you're supposed to do," she said, smiling in return as she handed him a fresh napkin and a heaping dish of pie and ice cream. "Eat."

"I wasn't talking about the pie," said Logan, watching her smooth lips.

Dawn flushed slightly but she didn't withdraw when he ran a fingertip over the back of her hand. Logan saw her color and the sudden tiny tremor in her hand beneath his fingertip. It was easy, so easy, for him to spread the lures leading to the sensual trap, because each lure was also the truth. He liked seeing her mouth soften when he smiled. He wanted to nibble on her lips more than he wanted to taste the rich, sweet juices of the pie. "I was talking about your lips."

"Feeling frisky, aren't you?" asked Dawn wryly, trying to subdue the leaping response of her body at the thought of having Logan's tongue tracing her mouth. She had dreamed of his skilled sensuality often enough before she came back to the Lazy W. But since she had been here, her own hunger for Logan had been like wires tightening within her, slowly, inexorably, tightening and bringing every nerve in her body to full awareness of his male presence. Knowing that he was nearly well and that he watched her body with masculine hunger wasn't helping her control her thoughts, either. "Nibble on this, cowboy."

Logan's mouth curved just short of a smile as he cut into the tender crust of the pie with his fork. "Where's your pie?" he asked innocently.

Dawn looked down at the tray with its two separate plates of pie à la mode and groaned. "You wouldn't."

"Sure I would," he said, licking up a stray flake of crust from his lips. "Try me," he murmured. "Please."

"Just a bite?" she asked, looking longingly at the untouched piece of pie.

"All right," he conceded. "Just one."

Dawn picked up her fork and began to cut into the pie, only to have Logan grab her wrist.

"But you said I could have a bite," she protested.

"Of me, not the pie."

She looked at Logan's mouth and was suddenly shaken by temptation. "Logan—" she breathed.

"It's all right," he coaxed, his voice low and very male. "This time I won't bite back."

He saw her eyes darken and her heartbeat surge wildly against the satin skin of her throat. For a moment she swayed toward him. Then she closed her eyes and drew back.

"I'm not up to your weight," she said, her voice haunted as she remembered his expertise and her own inexperience.

Logan's lips curved into a crooked smile. "I doubt it. I doubt it all to hell."

Before she could ask what he meant, his grip shifted to her braid. He tugged her forward gently but firmly, offering her no escape.

"If not a bite," he offered, "then a taste. Just a taste."

Dawn found her lips brushing over his, felt the outrush of his warm breath, tasted the tart-sweetness of cherry pie as his tongue followed her silent intake of breath into her mouth. For a wild moment she knew only his scent, his closeness, his warmth. When he drew back she had to control a small sound of disappointment.

"See?" he murmured. "No teeth, no claws, nothing but a little taste. Better than medicine any day."

"I don't think Dr. Martin would agree with you," said Dawn, her voice strained.

Logan simply watched her as he resumed eating the warm, fragrant pie. "You going to weave tonight?" he asked between bites.

For an instant Dawn resented the fact that he could so easily dismiss a caress that had her all but trembling in the palm of his hand. Then she realized that she was being unfair. Logan was simply teasing her because he was bored, and she rose to the bait every time. He had no way of knowing how inexperienced she was and what even his most casual touch did to her.

"Does the sound of the loom bother you?" she asked.

He shook his head. "I like it."

Dawn let out a long sigh. "Good. Mary Sue hated it. I could never weave when she was home. Of course, she wasn't home much." Then Dawn realized that she had brought her mother into the conversation and wished she had bitten her tongue. Even the mention of Mary Sue's name seemed to be enough to trigger Logan's anger.

Logan frowned at the resonances of an unhappy past that he heard in Dawn's voice. His fork hesitated on the way to his mouth as he remembered what Dawn had been like as a child—thin, haunted, lonely, caught in a web not of her own weaving. But now she was grown, the image of her mother, a living reminder of why Joe had died too young.

The sweetness of the dessert spread through Logan's mouth. Suddenly he didn't want to think about the past for a while. He simply wanted to be in the present, eating his favorite pie topped by his favorite ice cream, watching the most beautiful woman he had ever seen weave graceful patterns through the evening while he talked with her or was silent as the mood took him.

"What will you weave now?" asked Logan, gesturing with his fork toward the empty loom. "More curtains?"

Dawn let out a long, silent sigh of relief that he had chosen a neutral topic instead of delivering the sardonic verbal blast she had come to expect whenever Mary Sue or Joe came into the conversation.

"No," said Dawn, smiling at Logan with unknowing radiance, thanking him without words for not lashing out at her. "I'm going to do a tapestry."

That surprised Logan. "With knights and dragons and fair, fainting maidens?" he asked, more curiosity than sarcasm in his voice.

Dawn's laughter was as soft as the lips that had so recently brushed over Logan's. "Not quite," she said, fighting the temptation to kiss the dimple that appeared at the left side of Logan's mouth whenever he smiled in a certain way, as he was smiling now. "Tapestry is a weaving technique, not a blueprint."

Without missing a beat, Logan scraped his dessert plate clean and reached for the small piece of pie that should have been Dawn's. She groaned. He held out a forkful of pie. She reached for it, only to have it withdrawn.

"Fair's fair," he murmured. "You fed me for three days. Now it's my turn."

"But I'm not sick," she said, then realized wryly that if Dr. Martin could take her pulse and listen to her breathing right now he'd have her in a hospital. Or a padded room.

"My way or not at all," said Logan.

Dawn opened her mouth and felt the cool tines of the fork brush her lower lip as he neatly fed her a bite of pie. He watched her intently, making her feel wildly self-conscious as she licked her lips. She wondered if he had been similarly affected when she had fed him, if he had felt intimacy like an electric current with each bite of food taken from her hand. It was the way she felt with him now, a closeness that was almost unbearable.

"That's enough," she said. Her voice was unusually husky, caught between music and an emotion close to fear.

"One more," he said, watching her with eyes that were darker now, the pupils wide and very black against the golden brown iris.

Helplessly Dawn parted her lips, felt the smoothness of the fork and tasted the sweetness of the dessert. He watched every movement she made as she took the food he had given her. When she finished eating he tugged her close again, using the silky rope of her braid.

"I won't bite," he promised in a deep voice. "I just want to know—" His words stopped as he found her lips and traced their curves with the tip of his tongue.

She made a soft sound as his tongue slid between her lips, taking whatever words she might have said in protest. For a few moments he held her, knowing only her heat and the telltale shiver of her body when his tongue stroked hers. Slowly he released her.

"Now I know," he said. "Everything is sweeter from your lips."

Dawn closed her eyes and fought to control the sudden, overwhelming rush of her blood. Her vulnerability to Logan's smallest touch appalled her. How could she help him to understand the past if she couldn't even control her own responses in the present? Watching Mary Sue had taught Dawn and Logan to view sex as a weapon. If she succumbed to sensuality, she would lose whatever hold she had on Logan.

"I—" Her voice broke. She swallowed and tried again, but Logan was faster.

"Don't worry, darling," he said, his tone both soothing and amused. "Even if you're willing, I'm hardly able, am I?" He touched her lips with his fingertip when she would have protested. "Now tell me about this unknightly tapestry you're going to weave."

For an instant Dawn didn't know whether to be grateful or irritated that Logan could so easily dismiss the sensual tension between them.

You'd better be grateful, she reminded herself. *You're playing way out of your depth—and he knows it!*

Dawn went quickly to the loom, her gratitude increasing with each step away from Logan's deceptively lazy sensuality. She grabbed the topic of weaving and stuck to it grimly, determined to cage the prowling hunger of the moment.

"See how close together I've laid the warp yarns?" asked Dawn, looking at the loom rather than at Logan.

"Yeah, I noticed. Looks like you're going to have a hell of a time weaving anything in. The stuff is about solid."

"The harnesses will get a workout," she agreed, stroking the taut warp with her fingertips as though it were a harp. "Notice anything else different?"

He stared at the warp, humoring her. "All one color," he said laconically. "Not like the scarf you wove for Turk."

"And Shorty and you."

Logan shrugged. It still irritated him that she had woven a scarf for Turk, the black-haired ladies' man who was also the best hand on the Lazy W.

"The warp is all the same color," said Dawn hurriedly, wanting to bring back the warm, teasing intimacy of a few minutes ago, "because none of it will show."

Logan looked from the gauzy open-weave curtains where every warp yarn was revealed, to the densely laid warp on the loom. "Be kind of tough to hide all that, won't it?"

"That's what the tapestry weave is all about. Weaving over the warp so that only the weft shows. All the color, all the design, all the textures are in the weft itself."

"So you can make all kinds of mistakes in the warp and it won't show?"

"Up to a point, I suppose so." Dawn smiled. "I never thought of it that way." *If only the past could be overcome like that. Ah, God, if only!*

As always, Dawn's smile transformed her face from serene to animated, hinting at the laughter and intelligence that lay beneath her unusual beauty. As always, the transformation fascinated Logan, showing him new facets of her appeal. For a tearing instant he wished that Dawn were only half as decent as she was beautiful. Even a quarter as decent. He heard his own nearly anguished thoughts and suddenly realized that if she hadn't been Mary Sue's daughter, he would be seeking marriage rather than revenge from Dawn.

The thought shocked him. He had never expected to marry because he knew he wouldn't be able to trust a woman to that extent. Yet here he was looking at Mary Sue's image and thinking of a lifetime of trust.

Wanting it. Wanting Dawn.

"And pack down the weft yarn very tightly as I weave," continued Dawn, not aware that she had temporarily lost and then regained her audience. "The sketch tells me when to switch colors."

"The sketch?" asked Logan, his voice both soft and rough as he made himself concentrate on weaving rather than on his aching and all but uncontrollable desire for Dawn.

"Just a minute," she said eagerly. "I'll show you."

She walked out, unaware that Logan watched her with hunger in his amber eyes, hunger tightening every muscle of his body.

"See?" she asked, returning quickly with a sketch the size of a dinner tray in her hand.

Dawn went over to the bed and sat unselfconsciously on its edge in order to show the sketch to Logan. It took him a moment to focus on anything other than the feminine curve of hip and breast so close to his hand. With an effort of will he forced himself to see the sketch itself. The lines were drawn over a grid that resembled graph paper. The design itself was composed of graceful curves and sweeps and swirls of color. The margins were filled with bits of yarn and notes in a code that he didn't understand.

His glance returned to the colored portion of the sketch. He realized that it was an impressionistic scene of darkness and light. No—black ice and fire. The base of the sketch was a turmoil of dark shades with only a few incandescent threads of scarlet as contrast. As his eye traveled up the sketch, the fiery colors became more prominent until the darkness was merely a memory, a base to support and enhance the dancing richness of flames. There was something growing within the flames as well, but he couldn't tell what it was.

"No questions?" she asked. "Usually when I show someone a sketch they say 'What is it?'"

"Whatever it is, it's beautiful," said Logan simply, his glance traveling from darkness to light, from icy turmoil to hot elegance, from bitter ice to blazing fire. "Do you weave a lot of these tapestries?"

"Whenever I can take the time from my bread-and-butter work. I love the freedom and challenge of designing my own weavings."

"Bread and butter?" asked Logan.

"Ponchos, scarves, shawls, place mats and napkins, that sort of thing. Small decorative wall hangings, too. They all sell quite well in the boutiques around Aspen."

"That's how you've been earning your living?"

"Sure." Dawn saw the disbelief on Logan's face and asked, "What did you think I did?"

"A lot of rich men ski at Aspen," he said bluntly, remembering the thoughts that had tormented him when Kathy told him that Dawn was living in Aspen. "I assumed you, er, *skied* with them."

There was a moment of charged silence. Carefully Dawn reminded herself that she was going for a record—a whole day without arguing with Logan.

"Dawn," began Logan, oddly reluctant to argue despite his provocative remark.

"Once I have the sketch," she said with both determination and anger in her voice, ruthlessly interrupting whatever Logan had been about to say, "I have to dye some of the yarns. I could buy dyed yarns, but often they don't have just the precise shade in the weight or texture I need."

Logan settled back against the pillows, telling himself he was too tired to argue right now, knowing that was a lie. He had never felt less tired in his life. He simply didn't want to drive Dawn away. It was so pleasant to gently, deftly unravel Dawn's glossy braid as she talked. The strands were so smooth, so cool, as shiny as a raven standing in a pool of sunlight.

"Then what do you do?" he asked, looking up from the double handful of silky midnight he held, realizing that she wasn't talking anymore.

Dawn frowned over the sketch as she visualized textures and tones and the overall design that had both haunted and excited her for the past week. She didn't realize that her hair was spilling softly into Logan's hands, or that he had raised the cool strands to his face and was breathing in deeply, infusing himself with the fragile lemon-and-sunshine fragrance of her hair.

"Then I play with textures and densities," she said absently, deciding that she wanted the two figures in the center of the radiant sunrise to be more real, less abstract. They should contain something of the darkness from which they had arisen, too, instead of being creatures entirely of fire. Shadows would define them, as well as light. "Do you have a pencil?" she asked, turning suddenly toward Logan.

She stopped in shock as she saw him rubbing his cheek slowly against a double handful of her hair. He looked up, his amber eyes catlike in their depth and clarity.

"Have you ever woven anything using your hair?" he asked.

For a moment Dawn couldn't speak. "I—no," she said finally. Her voice was both throaty and musical, containing all the resonances of the emotions that were holding her motionless.

"Superstitious?" he asked.

"Of what?"

"Magic. Primitive people believe that if you give someone anything that was once part of your body, that person will have a magical power over you. Hair," added Logan, his voice deep, "is supposed to be particularly potent."

A visible shiver ran over Dawn as his words both caressed and threatened her.

"Weave a few strands of your hair into that design," he said huskily, touching the sketch with a caressing fingertip. "And then give it to me."

"You—you like the design?" she asked, closing her eyes in a desperate attempt to shut out the frightening attraction Logan had for her.

"Yes," he said, then added in a puzzled tone, "but I'm damned if I know why. That sort of thing generally leaves me cold."

"What sort of thing? Weaving?"

Dawn shivered as she sensed the shifting weight of her hair and knew that Logan was smoothing it over his skin as though it were cool water and he was burning. The memory of how the masculine, almost harshly drawn lines of his face had looked against the gleaming softness of her hair was like a fire burning darkly within her body. She didn't dare look at him again, adding to the sensual currents that flowed invisibly, hotly between them.

"Modern art," explained Logan, pouring her hair from hand to hand as though it were clear midnight water. "Abstract stuff. It has about as much appeal for me as a manure rake. Less, actually. I can use a manure rake."

Eyes still closed, heart beating too fast, Dawn smiled. Logan's hands wound more deeply in her hair as he saw the feminine response stirring within the smile. For a moment he struggled against an impulse to drag her down over his body and tangle himself in her sweet warmth as deeply as his fingers were tangled within her hair. All that allowed him to control himself was the fact that he wanted to seduce Dawn into admitting her desire for him. She had to want him and to show that wanting. Gaining that kind of power over her was more important than the temporary satisfaction of his male hunger. It was more than important. It was vital. Without that power he would be vulnerable to the same kind of sexual blackmail that had ruined Joe.

"If your art has to have a purpose, I suppose you could use my design to wipe your boots," offered Dawn, unconsciously tilting her head toward Logan, responding to the luxurious weight of his hands within her hair.

"No," said Logan slowly. "I'd hang it here, in the bedroom."

Her eyes opened. "Why?" she asked, surprised.

"There's something very sexy about that design," he said in a deep voice. He lifted a strand of her hair and teased her cheek with the silky ends. "That's why I like it."

Dawn felt color warm her cheeks. His perceptiveness startled her. She hadn't expected anyone but herself to realize that the heart of the fire was two lovers intertwined. She closed her eyes again, wishing that she hadn't felt the sensual promise in Logan's lips, heard it in his words, seen it in his fingers woven deeply into her unbound hair. Then she felt the warmth of his breath as he gently unclenched her hands and smoothed his lips across her palms.

"Will you?" he murmured.

"Will I—what?"

"Weave some of yourself into that design and give it to me."

She bit back a tiny moan as his teeth closed gently over the flesh at the base of her thumb. "Yes," she said, her voice too low, too soft, the voice of a woman promising more than she wanted to.

Logan's hands tightened around Dawn's. He wanted to peel back the sheet and feel her fingers on his naked skin, but it was too soon. Much too soon.

"Good," he said, forcing himself to release her hands. "Can I help?"

"Help," she repeated, opening her eyes.

He looked at their dazed green depths and smiled. "You spent a lot of time unwinding piles of yarn and rewinding it onto shuttles for those scarves," he pointed out. "I may not be able to bulldog eight steers in a row right now, but I should be able to wrestle a few handfuls of yarn."

Dawn's soft smile went through Logan like lightning through a storm. "What a wonderful idea!" She leaped to her feet. "Don't go away," she said, running lightly out of the bedroom.

His only answer was a short laugh that could have been a curse. "Not likely," he said to himself, looking at his sheet-draped body in disgust. "I'm a flaming invalid, remember?"

With each heartbeat his body stirred in silent contradiction, and his senses recalled the sweetness and silken pleasure of touching Dawn. He groaned softly. It was rapidly becoming a contest of wills as to who would seduce whom.

The thought shocked him. There could be no doubt as to who would win—not when losing meant being broken like Joe on the cold granite of a woman's heart.

Seven

Dawn returned from her own bedroom quickly, as though she were afraid Logan would change his mind about helping her. When he saw the size of the plastic bags she was dragging behind her, he groaned. The sound was echoed by a low mutter of distant thunder. The clouds, which had teased the mountains by day, had gathered into a spring storm after sunset.

"This was your idea," Dawn reminded him quickly, eyes bright with mischief. "I'd never take advantage of an invalid."

Logan gave her a sideways look out of hard amber eyes. "You're enjoying this, aren't you?"

For a moment she hesitated, uncertain about his mood. Then she smiled widely. "You bet your boots, cowboy. I love choosing the yarns, dying them, and weaving them. But unwinding, unsnarling, and rewinding skeins onto shuttles is borrr-ringgg."

Dawn skidded the bags across the floor and up against Logan's bed just as lightning sparkled briefly against the black windows. "It will be easier for you if you're sitting up," she said. Suddenly she frowned. "Do you feel well enough to sit up?"

Logan swore beneath his breath. He had spent almost every minute she wasn't with him pacing the room. He knew its dimensions to the last quarter-step. "I'm a man, not a baby," he said harshly. "I have more than enough strength to sit up."

"I'm sorry. I didn't mean—"

His curt gesture cut off her words. As he sat up, the sheet slid slowly off his chest and down to his waist. Dawn found herself watching the process with all too much interest. She told herself it was the artist in her that so enjoyed the blunt, muscular wedge of tanned chest contrasting with the egg-shell white of the sheets. It was the artist who wanted to trace the powerful lines of bone and sinew. It was the artist who wanted to stroke Logan in silent appreciation of the latent power beneath the masculine grace of his movements.

But it was the woman in her who wanted to rub her hands and lips over Logan's shoulders and chest. It was the woman who wondered if his skin would taste as smooth and warm as it looked. It was the woman who wanted to follow the darkly curling wedge of his hair as it became a single thick line disappearing beneath the sheet.

Lightning danced through the night, pulling thunder behind. The storm did nothing to settle Dawn's nerves. Blindly she thrust her hand into the yarn sack and brought out the first skein her fingers encountered.

"This is yarn," she said quickly.

Logan's mouth curved in male amusement. He had seen her curious, admiring glance slide down his body—and he had enjoyed it as much as she had.

"Do tell," he murmured. "Yarn. Fancy that."

Dawn's cheeks took on a warm rose shade. "Yes. Yarn," she said crisply. "Hold out your hands."

"Are you going to tie me up?" he asked, smiling and holding out his wrists like a man waiting to be handcuffed.

"Don't tempt me," she muttered, plucking at a trailing piece of yarn, trying to see if it was the single strand that would neatly unravel the skein.

"Does the thought of tying me up tempt you?" he asked, his voice dark, ruffling Dawn's nerves.

She looked up with wide green eyes, unable to conceal her shock.

"Didn't you know?" he asked, tugging gently on a long ribbon of her hair. "Some people like it that way."

"Tied up?" she asked in disbelief.

"Mmmmm."

"Do you?" she asked, only to flush as she heard her own words. The thought of Logan playing sensual games both fascinated and frightened her.

"Never tried it. Never wanted to. But if that's what it takes to turn you on—" A corner of his mouth tilted up. "I aim to please."

Dawn looked away hurriedly. She hadn't had nearly enough experience with men to handle Logan's teasing. "I don't require anything that strenuous," she said, the words tumbling out in her rush to prevent him from saying anything more. "Just space your hands so," she continued, adjusting his hands until they were about a foot apart, "hook your thumb over this end of the yarn and hold still."

The yarn was as black as her hair but not nearly so glossy. Once she had the first soft thick turns of yarn in place around Logan's hands, the unwinding went without a snag. He soon learned to move his hands gently from side to side, keeping a steady pressure while the yarn was pulled from the center of the skein.

As Logan worked he watched Dawn, puzzled by the conflicting signals she was sending out to him. Sometimes she watched him with a sensual hunger as great as his own for her. Yet when he moved toward her, she retreated. In another woman he might have put it down to inexperience. But not in Mary Sue Sheridan's daughter. If half the gossip were to be believed, Mary Sue had started sleeping with men when she was about fourteen. She had had Dawn when she was barely sixteen.

Besides, no matter whose daughter Dawn was, a woman who looked and smiled and walked like her didn't get to be twenty-one without being chased and caught by men. A lot of them.

Maybe she doesn't like sex, Logan thought as Dawn bent down and retrieved a shuttle as long as her arm from the sack. On the heels of that thought came another, Dawn shivering and burning in his arms three years ago. *No way she didn't like it with me. If she hadn't been a virgin she would have tripped me and beaten me to the floor that night.*

Then maybe she had a few bad rounds with men and decided to swear off sex for a while. So she's hungry, but she's not biting.

Maybe. And maybe she just learned how to tease.

Logan's eyes narrowed into dark amber slits at the thought. That's what Mary Sue had been best at. Teasing. Joe had warned him again and again never to put up with a tease. It had been years before Logan was old enough to understand what Joe had meant, but the lesson had been as thoroughly learned as Logan's lifetime aversion to whiskey.

Wind gusted against the window, bringing a light scattering of hail. Logan glanced at the black panes, then back at Dawn. With deft, elegant movements Dawn peeled the dark strands from his hands and transferred the yarn to a big

shuttle. The next skein she pulled out of the sack was a deep
wine color at one end. At the other end, wine shaded into an
oddly luminous midnight hue. Logan watched in fascination as the colors changed with each turn of yarn around his
hands.

"Is that one you dyed yourself?" he asked.

"You remember the shade of purple," she said ruefully,
remembering that some of the dye had ended up on her
shirt.

"On you it looked good."

"It would have looked better on a burgundy grape," she
retorted wryly.

Logan's mouth gentled into a smile. "Do you like wine?"

"Sometimes."

"When?"

"With dinner, after a long day of weaving," she answered. She found another shuttle and wound it full of the
changing darkness of the hand-dyed yarn. "Or sitting and
watching the fire with Prowl in my lap on a night like this
when it's stormy out." She shook her head slowly, sending
a silky fall of her hair over her shoulders. "I guess I'll have
to give up on that now."

"Wine?"

"Sitting with Prowl on my lap. Since she discovered the
barn mice she thinks she's found cat paradise."

Logan's mouth shifted into a definite smile. "I have a
small confession to make. Prowl isn't spending the night in
the barn chasing mice."

"No?"

"No. She spends it with me. Under the covers. Way under. Have you every slept with a cat tucked against the arch
of your foot?" Logan complained mildly. "Every so often
she mistakes my big toe for a kitten and starts washing it.
Tickles like hell."

Dawn laughed softly and murmured, "That explains it."

"What? One clean toe out of ten?"

"Nope. The hair sticking to the bottom of the sheets. I thought your feet must be as furry as the rest of you." Dawn's hands paused as she thought of all the tempting patterns of hair on Logan's body.

"Does it bother you?" he asked, sensing her hesitation.

"Hairy sheets?" asked Dawn, her voice husky, rippling with barely suppressed memories.

"No. Hairy men. Some women are put off by it."

Dawn looked even more shocked than she had when Logan had told her that men and women sometimes tied each other up for sport. "You're teasing me."

"Hell of an idea," he muttered. "Why didn't I think of that myself?"

"Logan, I'm serious."

"So am I," he said dryly.

She watched him for a long moment, seeing both the humor and the intensity in him. "Logan Garrett, I don't believe that any woman ever objected to anything as wildly sensual as the textures of a man's body. Especially yours!"

With a hungry sound Logan started to reach for Dawn to pull her into his arms, but the soft wine-dark yarn wrapped around his hands got in the way.

"Come here, darling," he said, holding his arms up and crooking his elbows so that she would fit between.

"Logan—" said Dawn, torn between desire and fear of that very same desire. He wanted her. She wanted to give herself to him. All that prevented her was the certainty that until Logan understood himself and her and the past, the most probable outcome of an affair between them would be a continuation of the past's wintry pattern of pain and destruction. She didn't want that. She wanted a time of healing for both of them. Only then could creation begin for them, a springtime of love melting the icy past.

"Don't worry," he coaxed. "I won't shed on you."

Dawn laughed helplessly, shaking her head. In the next instant she felt the shuttle being taken from her hands and Logan's arms looping around her. He toppled her onto his naked chest and felt both the shiver of desire and the stiffening of her body in its wake.

"What's wrong?" he murmured against her hair, rubbing his cheek over the sleek strands like a cat. "You know you want to touch me, so why are you trying to pull back?"

"I'm—I'm not used to this."

His laughter was a rough-edged purr. "Sure you are. You rubbed me down faithfully when the fever was bad."

"That's—different."

"Is it? Same man, same woman, same skin, same lovely hands. God, yes. Lovely," he said, moving his cheek against her skin. "I like being touched by you."

There was a long silence broken only by a muted rumble of thunder rolling down from the peaks. Finally Dawn sighed and let her hungry hands knead through the mat of Logan's chest hair to the muscle beneath. "Do you?" she murmured. "I've always wondered."

Logan lifted his head and stared at her serious green eyes. "You're not kidding, are you?" he asked, surprise clear in his voice.

She shook her head. Black hair rippled over him caressingly, making his breath wedge in his throat.

"I've always wondered if you would like being touched by me."

"Always?" he said gently, turning his lips against her arm.

"Six years. It seemed like forever to me. Especially after—"

Logan knew Dawn was remembering the night three years ago when he had nearly seduced her. A memory came to him—Dawn looking at him with curiosity in her eyes.

"Was that what you wanted to ask me three years ago? If I'd like to be touched by you?" he whispered, moving his mouth lightly from side to side on the inner softness of her arm. The scent of her was more potent than wine. Her lightest touch went through him like a shock wave, making him hot with desire. "The answer is *yes*," he said huskily. "Touch me, Dawn."

When she saw the lines of Logan's face drawn with an anticipation that was almost pain, she couldn't help touching her fingertips to his cheek, his mouth, the corded line of his neck. When her hand slid down onto the muscled slope of his chest and over the flat nipple concealed beneath a mat of dark brown hair, Logan's eyes closed and his breath hissed between his teeth. Instantly she snatched back her fingers.

His eyes opened, fierce and wild. "Stop teasing me and unwind the damned yarn from my hands," he said roughly. "I want to hold you properly."

"I don't—" Dawn's voice thinned into silence as the hunger in Logan sank into her, making her shiver with fear and sweetness. "It's too soon," she said desperately.

Amber eyes narrowed. "How long did you have in mind?" he asked with deceptive calm. But beneath the soft tone, anger curled. Part of it was at himself for being so vulnerable to her touch and part of it was at her for being who she was, Mary Sue's daughter. "A few days? A week? A month?" Then, as icy as the wind gusting outside the window, "Never?"

Dawn closed her eyes and hung on to the only truth she knew that might counter Logan's devastating attraction for her. "You aren't well yet," she said urgently. "You shouldn't even be thinking of—"

A flat crack of laughter cut off her words. "Around you, *thinking* is the least of my problems."

Logan gave her a long, brooding look, trying to decide whether the concern in her vivid green eyes was genuine or simply an extension of the sensual striptease. Either way, the answer to his hunger was the same: no. For whatever reason, she wasn't ready to come to him. And it had to be that way. Her coming to him. He wasn't going to follow her around on his hands and knees like Joe had Mary Sue.

No! It hadn't been like that! Joe hadn't been that kind of a weakling. He had been a man, not a spineless, whining—

Logan shuddered and wrenched his mind away from the much older brother who had been the center of his life. It had been Joe who raised Logan and Kathy after their father's stroke. It had been Joe who took over the running of the ranch when their parents moved to Denver in search of sophisticated medical treatment. It had been Joe who was always there until he had fallen in love with the wrong woman and tried to find solace in an endless whiskey river flowing through him.

"Logan?" asked Dawn softly, frightened by the bleakness that had come into his eyes, a reflection of the chill emptiness beyond the softly curtained bedroom window. "I'm sorry. I didn't mean to make you angry."

"It's nothing special. Sheridan women have a real talent for pulling my cork," he said curtly.

Logan lifted his arms from her. For long, long minutes there was no sound in the room but the erratic rattling of hail against the house and the whisper of yarn being transferred from his hands to the long, elliptical shuttle. Though the thought of talking about the past made Dawn clumsy with fright, she knew she had to take the chance. Being so close to Logan, yet so far from him, was tearing her apart.

"Kathy used to tell me how you were running the ranch by the time you were fourteen," she said softly.

"Joe ran the ranch until he died," said Logan. "I was eighteen then."

Dawn took a deep breath. "Funny how differently people remember the past, isn't it? Kathy said that from the time you were fourteen, if any of the hands needed anything, they came to you."

"And I went right to Joe," retorted Logan in a clipped voice.

How many times did you find him out cold, curled around a whiskey bottle? asked Dawn silently. If she had thought it would have done any good she would have repeated the question out loud, but she knew that Logan wasn't ready to hear it yet. He wasn't ready to hear anything about Joe that contradicted a younger brother's misplaced hero worship.

She put aside the full shuttle and lifted a new skein of yarn from the sack. The yarn was an eerie, almost iridescent blue-black. The texture was unusual, too, a combination of angora softness and unexpected knots. She plucked the trailing edge of the yarn skein and wound it deftly around Logan's hands before he could object.

"What do you remember best of your childhood?" Dawn asked quietly.

Logan gave her a narrow look but could see nothing beneath the elegant, maddening serenity of her face. He would have retreated from the discussion entirely if he could have. The darkly iridescent yarn being wrapped around his hands, holding him softly joined to her, made that impossible.

"Riding behind Joe is my first memory," said Logan curtly.

"How old were you?"

"Five. Maybe six. We were choosing a Christmas tree."

"Joe was—what? Seventeen?"

Logan nodded.

"It was nice of Joe to take you," said Dawn. "Most brothers would have considered a six-year-old to be a pest."

"Not Joe. He took me everywhere. Dad had just had his first stroke. Mom had all she could do to take care of him and keep Kathy out of trouble. She was barely a year old." Logan's eyes focused on the yard but he was seeing through it to a time when he had been young and Joe had been whole. "Joe didn't mind hauling me around. He taught me to ride, rope, brand, shoot—" Logan's lips curved into a crooked smile "—swear, and wear spurs without tripping over them."

A tremor of hopelessness went through Dawn as she heard the currents of affection and respect in Logan's voice.

"I thought he was half bear, half wolf, and all of God's sunshine rolled into one," admitted Logan. "Mom might be too tired to care and Dad might not know me at all, but Joe always had a smile and tall tale to tell me. It wasn't just me, either. Anybody needed a hand, Joe gave it to them. Down on your luck? Joe had a twenty for you. Need a shoulder to cry on? Joe would listen and never tell a soul. He should have been a minister. He loved everybody and everybody loved him."

Dawn saw the sudden fierce lines of Logan's face and knew what he was thinking. *Everyone but Mary Sue.*

"Well, not quite everyone," drawled Logan. "Your daddy thought Joe didn't own enough cows to be a real man. Your mama shined up to Joe right enough—until she saw the size of Sonny Sheridan's ranch. Then she decided it was more fun to be screwed by a man with a big ranch than loved by a good man with a small ranch. But the most fun of all was to leave Joe at the church with his new suit and shiny boots and egg all over his face."

The barely restrained hatred and overt fury in Logan's voice made Dawn's skin ripple uneasily. She had hoped that talking about the past might help to drain off some of the accumulated rage. Only then would Logan be able to feel something besides resentment when he looked at Mary Sue's image sitting across from him at breakfast and dinner. Only then would he be able to think of love rather than revenge.

But Dawn hadn't expected this. She hadn't expected to feel Logan's fury like a whip across her skin. She hadn't known how much it would hurt to see contempt make his eyes like amber ice as he looked at Dawn and saw instead the woman he had hated since he was old enough to understand that his beloved brother had been made to look like a weakling and a fool.

"Logan," Dawn said carefully, her voice husky with the effort of not crying out her fear, "memories are beautiful, but not always...true. At least, not all of the truth. I remember my grandmother Sheridan as being kind, wise, warm, patient, gentle. And she was, with me. With other people—" Dawn drew in her breath sharply "—with other people she was a stubborn old woman who never used a compliment when a sarcastic remark would get the same result. She was a half-Indian woman who had attended one of France's finest art schools. She was too proud, too educated and too intolerant of people who didn't see the world as clearly as she did."

"I thought you liked her," said Logan, his cold amber eyes measuring Dawn.

"I loved her!" said Dawn fiercely. "I still do. I'll love her until I die. That doesn't mean I'm blind to her shortcomings. People don't have to be perfect in order to be worthy of love." She closed her eyes, said a silent prayer and continued. "Like Joe. You loved Joe and he wasn't perfect."

"He was until he met Mary Sue," retorted Logan.

Dawn searched his eyes. "You can't believe that. A child might believe it, but you aren't a child anymore. People aren't ruined by a failed love affair. They can hurt each other, yes. They can wound each other terribly. But Mary

Sue couldn't have destroyed Joe unless he let her. Mary Sue dumped a lot of men and they not only survived, they lived to thank God that she was through with them."

"They weren't in love with her," snarled Logan.

"Love creates, it doesn't destroy," said Dawn urgently. "That's how you know it's love. Lust destroys. Lust and hatred and revenge. Look at Joe. Was it an act of love to drink himself to death?"

"Shut up!" snarled Logan. He grabbed her wrist with both his hands, stilling the movement of the shuttle. "Don't ever mention Joe's name to me again! Do you hear? *Never!"*

With a small sound, Dawn bit her lip and fought against the tears threatening her. The search for a pattern that would evoke Logan's ability to love rather than his ability to hate had led her into an argument neither he nor she could win. They could lose, though. They were losing now. Talking about the past didn't make it better.

It made it worse.

Logan felt the soft skin beneath his fingers and released Dawn as though he had been burned. Quickly she went back to work on transferring yarn from his hands to the shuttle. She desperately wanted to be finished, to avoid the storm that was gathering in Logan, waiting to score her with powerful, icy bursts.

She wasn't fast enough. Before the last of the black yarn was safely wound, he asked, "You ever see your parents?"

The question might have been merely polite but for the belligerence that drove the words as surely as the raw winds of April drove the racing storm outside. Dawn's hesitation was no more than a tiny movement of her hand. He saw it, though, just as he had seen everything about her in the past few days, watching her with an intensity that he recognized without understanding. He knew his question had disturbed her. That pleased him. He wanted to disturb her even as the hailstorm was disturbing the hopeful warmth of spring.

"I haven't seen them since I moved to Aspen," said Dawn.

"Why?" asked Logan. "Afraid your daddy will use you as table stakes in a poker game?"

As though she hadn't heard, Dawn put away the full shuttle and stared through the window at the wild dance of distant lightning. She told herself that she couldn't evade Logan's hostility toward her mother and herself any more than the warmth of spring could evade the last icy throes of winter. She had wanted to talk to him about the past and about his destructive hunger for revenge. But not like this. It hurt too much to see the man she loved look at her with contempt in his bleak amber eyes.

"That's what your dear daddy used to do," continued Logan relentlessly, his voice as deep as the thunder that growled against the gauzy curtains. "He'd get down on his money and start taking bids on your mama."

Dawn had heard the rumors even when she was in grammar school. They had cut her to the bone. She was older now. A lot older. It still cut her—not what her parents might or might not have done, but that Logan would use it against her.

"Maybe your brother should have learned to play poker," Dawn said, fighting to keep her voice neutral.

The silence was like the instant between lightning and thunder, violent energy waiting for the moment of release. And then it came.

"Want to know how much your daddy asked for you?"

"What?" she asked, whirling toward Logan.

"One thousand dollars." He watched her with narrowed eyes, seeing the color drain from her face as she realized what he was saying. "That's right, little girl. The night your daddy was bent on losing the Lazy W to me, I wouldn't pay a dime for your mama, so he tossed you into the pot. Said you were as good in the sack as your mama ever was. A thousand was your price. I turned him down. It was way too much to pay for a Sheridan woman. After you ran away from me, how many men did he sell you to before you decided to go into business for yourself in Aspen?"

Dawn fought to control the shudders of emotion rippling through her body even as thunder vibrated through the land. "Why are you doing this to me?" she asked hoarsely, thinking of Joe and afraid to say his name after Logan's warning. "What do you want from me?"

Logan's amber eyes narrowed as he measured the pain in Dawn's questions.

"The same thing I wanted three years ago," he said flatly.

"Revenge?"

"What else would I want?" he retorted.

Dawn closed her eyes, hoping that her despair didn't show through. "On me? Why? Beyond being Mary Sue's daughter, what have I done to you?"

There was no rational answer to that question and Logan knew it. The realization brought a fury as great as he had felt when he had listened to Mary Sue's image telling him that Joe had been weak rather than heroically wronged.

"You know, I've always wondered just what made you think you were too good to be my mistress," Logan said, his voice sardonic, cruel. "Was it the fact that your daddy was such a pillar of the community? No? Then it must have been that your mama was such a shining example of chastity. She was an angel, sure enough. Ask Joe. Oh, yeah. I forgot. You can't ask Joe. He died of an overdose of Mary Sue's kindness."

"Logan—"

But he kept talking, his words like sharpened steel, slicing into the inflamed past. "Mary Sue was so damned *kind* that when I went to her and told her Joe was dying and was calling for her, she laughed. She laughed and said she'd been through with Joe a long time ago, and now she would finally be rid of him, as well. And then she gave me a look out of those big green eyes, tossed back that black mane of hair and suggested that maybe we could get it on instead.''

Dawn wanted to let her own long hair fall over her face, concealing her shame. She could imagine what it had cost Logan to go to the woman he loathed and plead that she see his dying brother. Although it had happened years ago, the echoes of Logan's fury were still resonating in the room. Dawn finally understood the depth of the helplessness that Logan had felt; and she knew that it had been translated into a consuming need for revenge, a need to redress the balance of pain, to make Mary Sue finally understand what her shallow emotions had cost.

But Mary Sue would never understand. The revenge Logan wanted, the revenge he must have, was impossible, and Dawn couldn't bear any longer to watch the man she loved consumed by this unsatisfied hunger. Perhaps if he finally felt he had achieved vengeance he could put it behind him, could pick up the other threads of his life and weave a new, constructive pattern. If she could help him do that, any risk, any danger of hurting herself, would be worth it.

Somewhere underneath all that anger is a good man. Find him. Bring him home to us.

In a painful burst, Dawn realized how to help Logan. Make an end to it here, now. Find out what vengeance he wanted to take on Mary Sue's daughter.

And then let him take it.

''What would it take for you to feel that you've finally evened the balance between the Garretts and the Sheridans?'' asked Dawn, looking at the old loom rather than at Logan.

His breath came in sharply, soundlessly. He stared at the clean line of Dawn's profile, at the generous, unsmiling mouth and the soft rise of her breasts beneath her loose sweater. He had wanted her for years the way Joe had wanted Mary Sue, like hell on fire. Joe hadn't ever had the chance to exorcise his private demon.

But Logan would.

"You. As my mistress."

Eight

———

Dawn fought the fear rising in her, closing her throat. She had dreamed of being Logan's. But not like this. Revenge instead of love.

"All right," she said hoarsely. "When you're well—"

"No," Logan interrupted savagely. "I'll say when and where and how often. And you'll do what I say, or—"

"You'll strip me naked and leave me in the center of town," finished Dawn, her voice empty as she stared at the loom. "Yes, I know. You made that quite clear three years ago."

"Stand up," snapped Logan, his voice hard. He had called her Mary Sue's daughter, a tramp; and when Dawn had agreed to act the part he had felt a volatile combination of triumph and rage and hunger.

His narrowed amber eyes reflected both his contempt and his desire as Dawn slowly stood. Her jeans concealed the trembling of her legs, but nothing could conceal the chill of her hands or the pallor of her face as Logan reached beneath her sweater and casually fondled her breasts. When her only response was a small, strangled sound of protest, he yanked his hand out of her clothes impatiently. He was in the grip of the same wild passion that had hammered in his blood for years whenever he remembered Dawn's naked, softly curved breast peeking out from between strands of ebony hair.

"Take off the sweater," he said curtly. "The bra, too."

For a moment Dawn couldn't move. When she had agreed to become Logan's mistress, beneath her fear had been memories of his gentleness and passion when he had touched her three years ago. She hadn't realized that today he would take her quickly, casually, treating her like a prostitute.

That's what you are to him, Dawn reminded herself painfully. *A prostitute. And don't kid yourself. He's right. Your price wasn't money, but it was a price just the same.*

With tight, clumsy movements Dawn turned away to pull off her sweater.

"No," commanded Logan, his amber eyes watching the silky fall of her hair and the curve of her breasts against the wine-colored sweater. "Face me."

She closed her eyes and pulled off her sweater, letting it drop to the floor because her fingers were too numb to hold on to the soft folds. Her bra was much harder to remove. Its clasp evaded her cold fingers until Logan made an impatient sound and abruptly pulled her down across his lap. He peeled off her bra and took her mouth in the same instant, forcing her lips apart before she could regain her mental or physical balance. One large hand tangled in her hair, holding her still. The other fastened onto her naked breast, kneading it, demanding a response that she was too ashamed and frightened to give.

Helplessly, silently, Dawn wept. Her tears scalded across Logan's lips.

"What the hell?" he demanded. He lifted his head, looking at Dawn's eyes for the first time since she had said she would become his mistress. Her lashes were tightly closed and her skin was the color of snow. Tears flooded her cheeks and dripped onto her clenched hands. Beneath the ebony veil of her hair, her body trembled violently. "Look at me!"

Dawn twisted and hid her face in her hands, shaking her head, too ashamed to look at him.

"Knock it off," said Logan savagely. "You want me and you know it, or you wouldn't have agreed to be my mistress."

"I wanted you, but not like this," she whispered.

He moved with a speed and strength that shocked her. Between one breath and the next she found herself flattened beneath him. His naked body fitted intimately between her legs. His hard hands began unfastening her jeans quickly, efficiently.

"So we have to do it your way, do we?" he said tightly. "No passion on your part, just cold control. Make the man beg. You're just like your mother. A liar and a sexual cheat."

"No," said Dawn despairingly, but Logan didn't listen.

She felt her clothes being yanked away and knew that she was trapped in a pattern of her own weaving. Soon the man she loved would take in anger and revenge what she had wanted to give in love. When his hand came up between her thighs, probing her flesh with an intimacy she had never experienced, she bit her lip until it bled and wished she could die of shame.

Logan didn't see. He had eyes only for the soft perfection of her body. He remembered how exciting it had been to touch her three years ago. Her lack of response now infuriated him.

"Don't," he said threateningly when she shuddered and then lay utterly still beneath his hands. "I won't let you get away with the passive bit."

"What do you want from me?" she asked desperately, understanding only that whatever she did wasn't enough for Logan. He wasn't satisfied with his revenge. She gasped as his touch became even more abrasively intimate. Reflexively she tried to escape. He held her motionless with a strength that suddenly terrified her. She went rigid and wondered desperately how long she would have to endure this.

"Now what's wrong?" he snarled just as his mouth found the soft peak of her breast.

"N-nothing. Just—just g-get it over with, please!"

Logan's response was short and obscene. He lay on his side and glowered down at her tight, closed body. "For the love of God," he said, his voice thick with frustration and disgust. "Is this how Mary Sue taught you to act in bed?"

"She d-didn't teach me anything," Dawn said, her voice breaking. "If it's s-sexual acrobatics you want, you'll have to find another w-whore!"

The desperation in Dawn's voice reached through the hunger beating in Logan's blood. For a moment his hands stilled. Eyes closed, Dawn fumbled at the sheet, wanting to cover her nakedness and shame. Accidentally her hand grazed his hot male flesh. She snatched back her fingers, but not quickly enough. He had felt the iciness of her touch. It shocked him.

"What kind of game are you playing with me?" he demanded, his fingers closing around her arm.

"No game. I can't b-be anything but what I am," Dawn said, turning away from him, eyes tightly closed.

"A badly trained whore?" offered Logan sardonically.

A long shudder rippled through Dawn's body. "What do you expect from a virgin?" she asked, her voice empty.

Logan drew in his breath sharply. "Don't lie to me," he snarled, his voice icy, threatening.

"I'm not!"

He made a disgusted sound.

"Why don't you believe me?" she whispered.

"You're Mary Sue's daughter," he answered carelessly, but his eyes were vivid, utterly intent on Dawn.

"You're the brother of an alcoholic," she said, shaking with the force of holding in her emotions. "How many bottles do you have stashed in the closet? How many times has Kathy driven in and bailed you out of the drunk tank? How many times have you wallowed in whiskey and self-pity until—"

"Never." Logan's voice was like hail whipping over Dawn's unprotected flesh. "And I never will!"

"Don't you think I feel the same way about lust after watching my mother?" asked Dawn, her voice raw. "The thought of a man touching me like that makes my stomach turn over."

He saw the fear and shame in Dawn's face, heard the echoes of his own passionate rejection of alcohol and remembered her shivering with desire in his arms.

"You liked sex real well three years ago," he said bluntly. "Remember?"

"I thought it was love, not lust! Then I found out I was wrong. But I still—"

The rush of words stopped abruptly when Dawn realized what she had been on the verge of revealing. Logan wouldn't want to know about love. Not from Mary Sue's daughter. For a moment silence reigned in the room, only to be broken by a sudden fusilade of hail against the windows. Neither Dawn nor Logan heard.

"Finish it," he said, rolling her over until she had to face him. "Finish it or I will."

Dawn took a deep breath and tried to quiet the trembling of her body. She said nothing.

"You still wanted me, didn't you?" said Logan, triumph curling beneath his words. "No love, no sweet lies, nothing but good old lust. You're Mary Sue's daughter through and through."

A burst of hail rattled against the glass again. Dawn had a wild impulse to fling open the window and let the storm pour over her, washing her in ice, warming her. Sleet was softer, more gentle, kinder than the man who watched her with a lifetime of revenge gleaming in his eyes.

And Dawn watched him in turn, her eyes as wide and wild as the ice-haunted Colorado spring. Suddenly she rolled away from him again, back onto her side. She hugged herself, trying to warm her cold skin.

"I'm not lying to you," she said. "I'm a virgin. When you believe me you won't expect me to—to—"

"Have sex with me?" he said flatly.

"No," she said, her voice dull, defeated. "To pretend I'm enjoying it."

There was a long time in which the only sounds were Logan's curses and Dawn's attempts to control her broken breathing. His words were as hot as the tears he had felt falling on his lips just a few moments ago.

"Then why in hell did you agree to become my mistress?" he demanded finally.

"I wanted you to let go of the past," Dawn whispered. She took a deep, shuddering breath. "And—and a few minutes ago I didn't know the difference between seduction and rape. I do now."

The quiet, frayed words shocked away the last red haze of revenge and lust that had gripped Logan since the instant she had offered him the satisfaction of both. He suddenly realized that if she was as untouched as she had been three years ago, his handling of her just now had been at best coarse and unfeeling; and at worst, it had nearly been what she had called it. Rape.

Almost afraid to believe in Dawn's innocence, Logan stared at the tangled fall of her hair and the rigid line of her back, counted the shudders silently shaking her body. When he looked at her, he no longer saw the taunting jade eyes and black mane of the woman who had obsessed his brother. He saw Dawn's fear and inexperience and cursed himself for a fool. Now that she had offered herself, he wanted her more than he ever had, not less. He wanted her until it was all he could do to look at her smoothly curving hips and not take her right here, right now, easing a lifetime of rage and desire within her softness.

But she was shaking with fear of him. He didn't want her like that. He wanted her to tremble as she had three years ago, with passion. He wanted her to need him until she moaned with it, to welcome him into her untouched body with hungry little cries, to cling hotly to him with every bit of her sweet feminine strength.

"Come here, little leaf," Logan said in a husky voice. He gently gathered Dawn in his arms, tucking her hips and back into the curve of his body. He didn't force her to face him, for the echoes of her shame still rippled through her flesh. "It's all right," he murmured against the silky mass of her hair. "I believe you aren't experienced at all. I won't hurt you. Rape isn't my idea of how to treat a mistress for pleasure. Or even for revenge."

For a moment all Dawn felt was the shocking warmth of Logan's powerful body curving around her. Even before the meaning of his words sank into her mind, the difference in his touch reassured her. He no longer handled her with a callous travesty of intimacy. His fingers were gentle on her hair, her arms, and his embrace calmed rather than threatened her.

"L-Logan?" she whispered, her voice breaking, almost afraid to hope.

"Hush," he said softly, nuzzling against her hair until he found the soft curve at the nape of her neck. "It's all right. I won't hurt you."

Yet even as Logan tried to reassure Dawn, his arms tightened around her. He was afraid that she would sense his own regret at how he had treated her and turn his weakness against him. He was afraid that she would get out of his bed and run and keep on running, the way she had three years ago. But he knew he couldn't let her go. Not this time. Not when he was so close to having her.

"Just don't try to run away," he said, his voice rough with a hunger that he couldn't conceal. "It wouldn't do you any good. I'm not letting you go, Dawn. I'm holding you to your promise. You're my mistress now."

"I—I'm not backing out on our bargain," Dawn said, forcing the words past her lips. Whatever happened, whatever it cost, she knew she had to slash through the old pattern of revenge and hatred, ripping it from the past's unforgiving loom, making it possible for a new pattern to be woven. She loved Logan. Surely in the name of love she could overcome her fear of sex. "I'll be your mistress if you'll promise to make an end to vengeance."

Logan felt the shudder that took her body and wanted to curse, knowing it was fear rather than pleasure that had moved her.

"Dawn," he said, trying to be gentle. But the word came out almost harsh, ragged with need.

"Just be—" Her voice broke. She rolled over and looked at him with shadowed green eyes. "Just be gentle, Logan. At least the first time. Please. I won't ask anything of you that way again," she pleaded, remembering how he had reacted so violently to the idea of her controlling him sexually. "I don't want to make you beg. I'm just—afraid."

Logan closed his eyes, not wanting her to see the emotion in his own as he wondered what Joe would have given to have Mary Sue pleading softly in his arms. But Dawn wasn't her mother, and his brother was dead.

"I'll be gentle," Logan promised. Then he smiled crookedly and bent to brush his mouth over hers. "It's a good thing I'm not up to snuff."

"What do you mean?"

"It will make it easier for me to go slow," he admitted, pulling the covers up underneath Dawn's chin, hiding the smooth temptations of her body from his hungry eyes and hands. He propped himself on his elbow and caressed her cheeks with his fingertips. "There's no hurry," he said, lying through his clenched teeth as an innocent movement of her hips brushed against his rigid flesh.

Yet the words weren't entirely a lie. He wanted her to be as hot and nearly wild as he was. He wanted to take her virginal control and shred it so completely that she would never be able to refuse him again. He needed to know to the bottom of his mind that she wanted him too much to play cruel sexual games, driving him crazy until he would say anything, do anything, be anything in order to have her.

Like Joe with Mary Sue.

Savagely Logan pushed away memories of his brother's obsessive desire for a woman who had looked exactly like Dawn. Joe had never gotten what he wanted from Mary Sue. If he had, he would have been able to walk away from her.

I don't need to worry about that anymore, Logan told himself fiercely. *Dawn has been a fire burning in me for years, but I'm going to have her. And when I've had enough of her, the fire will go out and I'll be free.*

Yet Logan knew that simply having Dawn wasn't enough, or he would have taken her a few minutes ago. It wasn't just her smooth, elegant body he wanted. It was her passionate response and the wild little cries that echoed through his memories, feeding the flames of his hunger. He needed those cries. He needed to know that he, Logan Garrett, had called them out of the depths of Dawn's innocence. He needed to know that she was holding nothing back from him, that no matter who had her after him, there would be nothing new for her to experience with any other man.

Logan no more questioned his irrational need than he questioned the fiery lightning storms that stalked Colorado's uncertain spring. And he could no more control his need than he could the lightning itself.

"I'm going to kiss you," he said softly, nuzzling the line of Dawn's ear, inhaling the fresh scent of her hair. "That won't frighten you, will it? Just a kiss."

Dawn saw Logan's dark lashes lower over his eyes until not even an amber glint showed through. Her breath stopped as he brushed his lips across hers. But that was all he did, a simple, light caress of his mouth on hers. He didn't demand or seize the sweetness waiting behind her lips. The caress came again and then again, teasing her, haunting her, until her breath sighed out and her mouth followed his from touch to touch, silently asking for a more intimate kiss.

The tip of Logan's tongue traced Dawn's lower lip. At the first instant of contact she hesitated. He withdrew and returned to brushing his mouth over hers. The soft, nibbling caresses continued until hunger replaced fear in the tension of her body. She sighed and tried again to capture his teasing lips. This time she didn't retreat when his tongue caressed the sensitive line of her mouth. Instead she tried to move closer, to increase the pressure of the kiss. He retreated by increments until she was straining futilely beneath the straitjacket of the sheet he had wrapped around her. She could almost reach him, almost feel the firm sweetness of his mouth against hers—almost, but not quite. She made a frustrated sound.

"What is it?" murmured Logan, his voice soft and his hands unyielding as he pressed down on the covers around Dawn, gently and efficiently holding her against the mattress.

"I want—" she said, then broke off as his lips teased her once again.

"You want?" he encouraged huskily.

"I want you to kiss me."

"How do you want me to kiss you? Like this?"

Again the fleeting, butterfly caress of his warm lips over her aching ones.

"Yes, but—a little harder, Logan."

He hoped that she didn't feel the sudden tightening of his body at her revealing request. The last thing he wanted to do was frighten her again.

"Like this?" he murmured, carefully fitting his mouth over Dawn's.

For long moments Logan simply savored the feel of her lips, soft and warm, sweet and innocent. He rocked his mouth gently from side to side, changing the caress with each movement, making the kiss always different, always new. Despite his hunger to taste her, to feel her tongue moving against his, Logan didn't offer or demand greater intimacy.

"Like that?" he asked, lifting his head and looking down at the woman whose mouth even now sought his blindly.

Logan's breath came in suddenly, soundlessly. Dawn's eyes were closed, her lips flushed with his kiss, and the possibility of passion showed in her pulse beating softly, quickly, beneath the creamy skin of her throat. Her eyes were a flash of jeweled green as they opened. Almost helplessly she focused on his mouth.

"Logan..." The word was as much a sigh as a name.

"Yes, darling," he said and bent down to her mouth once again.

Dawn watched his mouth descend with infinite slowness. Her breath stopped, but not in fear. She was remembering a time three years ago when he had bent down to her like this and the sweet possession of his kiss had made her whole body shiver. She wanted that again. She wanted to feel his heat radiate through her, to see his eyes darken with passion until there was only a rim of molten gold remaining around the pupil.

This time when the tip of Logan's tongue traced Dawn's mouth she made a shivering, wild sound in the back of her throat and opened her lips, asking wordlessly for more of his touch. The sound and the response went through him in a passionate shock wave that all but shattered his control. Because he wanted her too much, he touched the inner softness of her mouth only once before withdrawing again.

The swift, gliding caress of Logan's tongue made Dawn hunger for more. He tasted so clean, so good, so warm. Without realizing what she was doing, she ran the tip of her tongue over her lips as though she were savoring the flavor of a fine wine. Logan saw, and lightning pooled hotly in his aroused body, lightning aching to be free. He bent down again and touched her pink tongue with his own, letting her taste spread through him. With quick, catlike strokes he licked the smoothness of her lips and the velvety roughness of her tongue.

Dawn slowly stopped straining against the confinement of the covers, for Logan was no longer just beyond reach, tantalizing her with his light kisses. He was filling her senses, gently crushing her against the bed as her lips opened willingly beneath his. With slow, sensual consummation he took her mouth entirely, cherishing her, leaving no surface, no texture, no soft secrets unexplored.

When his tongue thrust smoothly, completely, into her mouth, Dawn felt a strange tension curl in the center of her body. She wanted the kiss to be as deep and wild as the sensations shimmering inside her. She wanted to absorb the man she loved into herself, to melt into him, to join with him so completely that nothing could ever tear them apart.

The odd, ragged sound that came from Dawn's throat made Logan stiffen, afraid that he had frightened her again. With agonizing slowness he separated his mouth from hers, feeling as though he were peeling away his own living skin. She arched up against the covers, fighting them, wanting him.

"Easy, darling," he said hoarsely, reining in the passionate hunger that raged through him. "It's all right."

"No, it's all wrong!" Dawn said, the words tumbling out so quickly that they were almost unintelligible. Her luminous eyes searched his face, his eyes, his sensuous lips as she struggled to free herself from the unwanted cocoon of covers. But she couldn't get free, for his arms were resting on either side of her, pinning her in place. "Oh, Logan, aren't you even going to let me hold you?" she asked raggedly.

She didn't understand the relief that showed on his face as he shifted his weight, freeing her. The dusky pink tip of her breast was revealed as her arms struggled out from beneath the covers and around his neck. With a groan Logan bent down and brushed his lips across her nipple as he had brushed across her mouth—gently, hauntingly.

For an instant Dawn froze. She looked at Logan in shock, but he didn't see her. His eyes were closed, his face intent, almost pained, as he savored her warmth and softness against his lips. The naked intensity of his expression stopped the protest forming in Dawn's throat.

And then the moment for protest was gone. She was lost to the beauty of his thick lashes lying across his tanned cheek, to the bronze richness of his hair contrasting with her creamy skin, to the stunning sensuality of his tongue cherishing her breast.

When Logan felt the sudden tightening of Dawn's nipple against his tongue, the ache of his hunger hardened until it was both pain and pulsing pleasure. He had dreamed of caressing Dawn like this, of feeling her innocent, uninhibited response; he had dreamed, but he hadn't even guessed how sweet it would be. With a groan that was more felt than heard, he drew both the hardened nipple and the satin smoothness of her breast into his mouth. He suckled her rhythmically, not quite gently, and was rewarded by the small sounds of passionate surprise that rippled from her. Her breath came quickly but her hips moved with slow, ancient instinct, seeking him in rhythms that matched his caressing mouth.

It cost Logan every bit of control he had to slowly, slowly, release Dawn's breast. And then he nearly came apart when he saw her watching his mouth cherishing her, watching his tongue as it returned again and again to the tight rose crown of her nipple. The sheet lay diagonally across her breasts, concealing half of her beauty. The knowledge that she was naked beneath the sheet made his body clench with hunger. He had never touched a woman half so beautiful, a tenth so responsive. She was no longer embarrassed or afraid of his intimate caresses; she was glorying in them. There was a sensual flush beneath her skin as she watched him, and her lips were glistening, parted, waiting to be filled. The thought that the rest of her body might be waiting just like that for him was like a sweet knife sliding into him and turning slowly, hotly.

He closed his eyes because he could not look at her any longer without taking her.

"Logan?" breathed Dawn, easing her fingers deeply into his hair. She couldn't help the throaty sound of pleasure she made as he rubbed like a great cat against the pressure of her hands. But still he didn't open his eyes, didn't open his mouth to take the taut breast that was almost brushing his lips, silently begging to be caressed again. "What is it?" she asked hesitantly. "Am I doing something wrong?"

He gave a harsh crack of laughter. "Oh God, darling, if you did any better I'd be all over you like thunder over the mountains."

The thought of being surrounded by the unleashed power of Logan's passion should have frightened Dawn, but there was no room left in her for fear—he was kissing her dusky rose nipple again, cherishing her with a hunger that made her moan. She felt the moist heat of his mouth at the same instant that the sheet began slowly retreating down her body. The sheet stopped just short of revealing her other breast completely, showing only the firmly rounded upper curve and the nipple that was even now tightening in sensual anticipation. She waited with breath held and eyes closed, wanting to know again the shimmering beauty of Logan's caress. He sensed her tension and looked up to find her eyes closed, her expression almost strained. With swift, gentle hands he pulled her hair forward and let it fall across her breasts, wholly concealing them.

"You're so beautiful," he murmured, stroking her body slowly, coaxingly. Each stroke stopped short of her aching breasts. "There's nothing to be shy about."

"Logan, you're torturing me," she said raggedly.

"Am I?" he asked. His lips curved into a very male smile. "I don't mean to. Tell me what I'm doing wrong."

"You're not—you're not touching me," she said in a rush.

"You sure?" he asked, his breath caressing her as he brushed his mouth over her lips. His hand stroked her shoulders and her arms and her cheeks. "I'm touching you," he said, his voice rich with a lover's warm laughter. "See?"

The teasing intimacy of Logan's smile both pleased and frustrated Dawn. "That wasn't what I meant."

"Then what did you mean?" he asked, kissing her lightly on her nose.

"I want you to—to—"

Logan saw the blush sweeping over Dawn's clear skin and remembered that despite her response to him she was very new to sensual games. He took her mouth in a single, sweet motion that made her forget her sudden embarrassment. Slowly his fingers parted the silky black veil of her hair to find the breast beneath. He caught the nipple between his fingers and tugged, making her gasp deep within her throat.

And then she gave him the words he had hungered for.

"Yes," she sighed against his mouth. "Oh yes, Logan. That's what I wanted. I just didn't know how to ask."

Dawn arched against his knowing fingers, not noticing that the sheet had slipped down to her waist with the sudden movement of her body. When his hand tightened on her back, lifting her to his hungry mouth, she didn't object. She wanted the wild sweetness of his tongue. She needed it. And she told him with every cry, every tiny arc of pleasure-pain she gave him as her nails dug unknowingly into his skin.

Slowly Logan eased Dawn back onto the bed, caressing her. His teeth raked tenderly over her taut nipples, sending heat rippling through her body. Her hips moved in instinctive sinuous response, making his breath come out in a tearing groan as he felt control slipping away. Whether she knew it or not, she wanted to feel him sliding into her body, filling her, moving inside her with every bit of hard passion she had aroused in him. His hand caressed the length of her smooth skin, dragging aside the sheet, returning to slide between her thighs until he could touch the softness and heat hidden there.

The intimacy of Logan's touch shocked Dawn. Instinctively she moved away, closing her body against his caress. The withdrawal snapped Logan's strained control. With a single savage curse he pinned her to the bed.

Nine

Logan saw the panic darkening Dawn's eyes and felt it in the sudden tension of her body. He realized that she hadn't been teasing him, leading him on only to refuse him when his body was rigid and clawing at him with unsatisfied need. She was simply, literally, untouched by any man but him. Everything he did to her was new, an intrusion into a physical privacy that was as old as Dawn herself.

Though hunger clawed through Logan, his mouth was gentle as he kissed her. "Let me touch you," he whispered. "I won't hurt you, I swear it. Just let me touch you. There's no reason to be shy with me," he murmured deeply, his voice as seductive as his hands caressing her breasts, as hot as his tongue licking her into taut peaks once again. "I'm going to know every sweet, straining bit of you like this," he promised, smoothing over her skin with delicate care. "You can blush and you can plead but in the end you'll be crying for me. I promise you, Dawn. You'll cry for me just like my body's crying for you.''

Slowly, firmly, Logan's hands moved back down Dawn's body. This time he didn't throw aside the sheet. His hand slipped beneath it. Dawn waited in an agony of suspense while his hard, warm palm caressed her stomach, her thighs, her calves, her hips. Each time he approached her soft, secret flesh she stiffened. His mouth found her breast again, tugged it with slow, sensual rhythms that were matched by his hand sliding over her skin. After a time she forgot to be afraid, forgot to be shy, forgot everything but the liquid fire that was coiling tightly between her legs and running like lightning through her body.

When his hand brushed over her tangled black curls she gasped, but not in embarrassment or fear. His lightest touch sent a wild shiver of anticipation through her. She wanted something more than his fleeting, teasing caresses, something she had never known. His gentle, maddening fingers returned, tracing incandescent patterns on every bit of her except the hidden, aching softness. When he ruffled her midnight hair again, her slender legs moved restlessly, opening slightly, inviting a more intimate touch.

Logan couldn't control his shudder of response at the silent feminine plea. His fingers slid delicately into the warm tangle of her hair. Slowly he traced fragile patterns on her most sensitive flesh. She moved with him gracefully, seeking his fingertips as she had once sought his lips. With a husky sound of need he bent his head and dipped his tongue into her navel. The unexpected caress made Dawn moan his name. Her knee flexed in sensual surrender as she moved blindly against his hand, yielding even more of herself to him.

When Logan felt her satin heat answer his caress, he groaned and deepened the touch as he had longed to do. It wasn't enough. He wanted to taste her, to move inside her, to hear his name a broken cry on her lips. But it was too soon, too soon. Even the gentle seeking of his fingers had surprised her in the instant before passion reclaimed her reflexes, yielding the softness of her body to him once again.

Slowly Logan touched Dawn more deeply and then more deeply still, letting her adjust to the fact of a man within her body. He gentled her with words and caresses when she would have retreated. Her shyness no longer angered him, for he knew now beyond all doubt that Dawn was a virgin rather than a tease.

The knowledge reassured him, telling him that he hadn't been a fool to believe her shy and yet passionate acceptance of him. It inflamed him to know that within a few minutes his touch had transformed her response from virginal shock and fright to an incandescent sensuality that was sending him right up to the edge of his control and leaving him hanging there in an agony of pleasure. He was grateful that she was too inexperienced to want to touch him as he was touching her. Just the thought of her sweet, hesitant hands on his body made him groan. The reality would have made him burst.

His teeth rasped gently along her thigh as his hand claimed her swiftly, deeply, wanting her, shaking with his wanting. He felt her suddenly tightening around him and he was afraid that he had frightened her again.

"Dawn—" Logan's voice was hoarse as he lifted his head to look at her.

Dawn's eyes opened, and their color was a green so intense that Logan knew the answer to his unasked question before she spoke. But he waited anyway, wanting to hear her, wanting to savor each husky resonance of passion in her voice.

As she looked at him she wondered at the harsh expression on his face. Then his hand moved again and she felt pleasure cascade through her, tightening her body until she didn't think she could bear it anymore. He found the tight, incredibly sensitive nub of flesh hidden within her softness and stroked it. She trembled and cried out, arching sensually as he took her body from her control. He removed his touch with tormenting slowness and she cried out again.

"Logan?" she asked raggedly. "Logan?"

"Anything," he murmured against the hot skin of her thigh. "Anything at all."

"Am I supposed to—to ache?"

A shudder ripped through him. "Where does it hurt, darling?" he asked huskily. "Tell me. I'll kiss it and make it well."

Dawn's eyes widened in shock and a sensual curiosity that she couldn't conceal.

"Here?" he asked, tracing Dawn's flushed, slightly bruised mouth with his finger.

Her lips opened beneath the teasing pressure. He touched the tiny serrations of her teeth and felt her tongue move slowly, moistly over him.

"Is that where it hurts?" he asked, his voice so husky it was almost rough.

She shook her head slowly, and each movement was a caress over his sensitive fingertip.

"Here?"

He touched the tight peak of her breast with his damp fingertip and was rewarded by a sudden intake of her breath.

"A little," she said softly, watching his lips come closer to her.

"Just a little?" he asked, his mouth hovering so close that he could sense the racing of her blood beneath her skin.

Her answer was lost in a tiny cry as her nipple hardened almost painfully beneath his caressing mouth.

"Better?" he murmured, then moved down her body before she could answer. "Here?" he asked, blowing teasingly into her sensitive navel. He kissed her slowly, drawing a sigh and a murmur of pleasure from her. "All well now?" he asked, lifting his head and watching her. "No more aches?"

"I—" Her voice broke, caught between inexperience and need. His smile made her breath catch. His hand slid down until she forgot what she had been trying to say.

"There?" he asked softly.

Sensual lightning ripped through Dawn as Logan's head bent over her again. She called his name, but all that came out was a moan as he found the aching focus of her desire. He cherished her with a sweetness that made her forget her innocence, forget her fear, forget everything but the wild pleasure of his touch. Her body tightened in instinctive anticipation, gathering itself for the moment of release.

Logan moved again, lying between Dawn's parted legs, stilling the wild trembling of her body. He found the satin heat of her, drawing out a moan as her legs moved to hold him as tightly as her arms were. He touched her again lightly, drinking in the passionate shivering of her body.

"Look at me," he murmured, teasing her now with his hungry male flesh rather than his hand. "Watch it happen. For both of us."

Dawn looked up into Logan's eyes, seeing and feeling and sharing the sliding, incandescent instant when two became one. The intensity of his response shuddered through her, through him. His face had a taut, almost agonized expression that turned her heart inside out. Then the sweet, moving pressure of his possession shimmered through her and she closed her eyes against the tears she couldn't control.

"Am I hurting you?" he asked, his voice rough with the effort it took not to simply give in to the smooth, tight, incredible perfection of being buried within Dawn.

"No," she said softly, and the word was a sigh of ecstasy that rippled through her, tightening her around him even more. She arched slightly, moving over him in turn "Logan, it feels—it feels so *good*."

"Oh God, darling," he groaned. "I know."

As Logan bent to kiss Dawn, he moved within her. She let out her breath in a husky moan and arched against him again, giving herself to him with a sweetness and trust that nearly undid him. She came to him again and again, breathing his name and her wonder at the wild pleasure racing through her, a pleasure she had never known until he touched her, moved inside her, taught her that she had been born for this day, this instant, this man. The waves of rippling ecstasy became closer, hotter, harder, matching those of the man making love to her, pouring himself into her as she cried out and came apart beneath him.

For a long time Logan lay heavily against Dawn, utterly spent. Her warm breath caressed his neck and her heart beat beneath his lips as he savored the smoothness of her throat. A new feeling spread slowly through him, a radiant peace that was unexpected and achingly sweet. He found himself wanting to hold time in place, never to go on from this instant of feeling Dawn warm in his arms. He had spent his life frozen inside winter and never even known it until spring had come to him innocently, generously, melting away years of ice to reveal the possibilities of life beneath.

Logan nuzzled Dawn's cheek and kissed her eyelids. The taste of her tears shocked him. He remembered the moment he had taken her and she had wept. And he remembered that he had promised not to hurt her.

"I'm sorry, little leaf," he said, easing from her body but not from her arms. As he did, he saw the unmistakable brightness of Dawn's blood on himself. He rolled onto his side and gathered her close, realizing anew how small she was against him, how strong he was by comparison. No wonder she had been frightened of him. "I didn't mean to hurt you," he said, his voice husky and his eyes haunted as he remembered how close he had come to taking her without any gentleness at all.

Dawn watched him with eyes that were luminous, deep, utterly at peace. "You didn't hurt me," she whispered.

"You cried. You're still crying."

"Haven't you ever cried because something was too beautiful to bear?" she asked softly.

Logan shook his head. "No."

Yet even as he spoke he felt a strange emotion closing his throat and burning behind his eyes. *Dawn is like that. Too beautiful to bear.*

And on the heels of that realization came a winter wind, freezing him. He had believed that if he took her he would be free of her. He wasn't. He was more deeply entangled in her than ever. More vulnerable. She could take his need for her and tie him in knots with it, strangling him as Mary Sue had strangled Joe. It was Dawn's blood that had been shed today. Tomorrow or the next day or the day after it would be his own blood draining away. Like Joe's had. Would she be like Mary Sue? Would she watch a good man bleed to death and smile?

Like mother, like daughter.

Like brother, like brother?

Like hell! Logan snarled silently. *Dawn is my mistress, period. I'm in control, not her. She does what I want when I want it. That's the way it is and that's the way it will stay.*

And right now Logan suddenly wanted as much distance as he could get. He had sunk too far into Dawn, and she into him. He could never be wholly free again, and he knew it at some primitive, wordless level. The knowledge was another whipping winter wind, freezing him, telling him that he was trapped in a situation that could lead only to his own ruin.

Dawn sensed the change in Logan as she tried to snuggle closer to his warmth. Where he had cradled her a moment ago, now he turned his back on her as though he couldn't bear to touch her.

"Logan?" she asked softly, caressing his shoulder without realizing it, drinking in the warmth and strength of the man she loved. "You didn't hurt me," she repeated, not understanding why he had withdrawn. Her lips brushed against the bunched muscles of his back. Her breath caught as she remembered what it had been like to watch him become part of her, to know that he was as intensely moved by that joining as she had been. "It was...unbelievably good."

Logan felt the rapid, violent stirring of his own body as her husky confession and soft caresses raced through him. His helpless response to Dawn was a betrayal of everything he had ever believed about himself. He wasn't like this with women. He wasn't like this at all, period. He had always controlled himself because he had grown up watching the terrible cost of not being in control. Yet here he was, too sick to put in a full day's work, and all Dawn had to do was touch him and he was hard again, hurting, wanting her like hell on fire even though the sweat hadn't dried on his body from the last time he had taken her.

Maybe Joe had been the lucky one after all. He never knew what he was missing.

"Get out of my bed," said Logan, his voice cool, icy. He jerked up the sheet, concealing his uncontrollable physical response to Dawn. He heard the sudden intake of her breath, felt her hand freeze on his shoulder. "Playtime's over."

"But—"

"Out." Logan's voice was clipped. He turned suddenly and stared over his shoulder at Dawn. The confusion on her face almost stopped him. Then he remembered Joe's wasted life. The words came quickly after that, easily, cruelly. "On-the-job-training is bad enough. I sure as hell don't need a mistress who doesn't know enough to make herself scarce when the sex is over with.''

For a moment Dawn couldn't believe what she had heard. Then the echoes of the words burst in her mind. She felt first cold, then hot, and knew that her shamed flush showed from her naked breasts to the widow's peak on her forehead. Without a word she left Logan's bed and his room, shutting the door behind her.

As she went down the hall she waited for the tears to come. They did not. All that came was a chilling sense of loss and betrayal. She lay down on her bed and stared at the ceiling, seeing the pattern of her own appalling stupidity. She had forgotten her own fears, forgotten the hard lessons of the past, forgotten everything but the ecstasy of having the man she loved surround her with his gentleness and passion.

Even now the memory made liquid fire curl through her, a haunting need that made her ache.

With a sound of despair Dawn closed her eyes. She loved Logan. She had promised to be his mistress, and as she promised there had been hidden deep within her the hope that once she had given herself to him without reservation he would trust her. He would know that she wasn't cruel in the way that her mother had been cruel with Joe. Mary Sue had used loveless passion to control men. Dawn had risked the destructiveness of passion with a man who didn't love her. When Logan had come to her so gently, so exquisitely, she had thought he understood that her response had been a gift to their future rather than an installment payment on the debt of their past.

She had been wrong. Logan understood only the past. Revenge. When she had given her word that she would be the recipient of that vengeance, she had believed that she could teach him the healing beauty of love. Instead, he had taught her the terrifying, unspeakable beauty of physical passion.

Dawn knew that she would go to Logan again if he wanted her, that she would give herself to him and pray that he would take as much joy in her as she did in him, that there finally would be an end to vengeance and a beginning to love. If not the next time they made love, then the next, or the next. She could not refuse him because she had never been so alive as when he was deeply inside her, moving with her, his dark voice telling of her beauty and his own potent need.

Oh God, Dawn screamed silently, horrified at the sensual hunger uncurling and prowling through her body with mindless power. *I'm no better than my mother after all!*

Dawn closed her eyes and shuddered soundlessly, chilled to her soul at the stark pattern she saw condensing out of the past.

After a long time she pulled herself off the bed, showered and dressed with clumsy fingers. She had supply lists to write out, clothes to wash and mend, a thousand details calling out to her. Love or vengeance, creation or destruction, life pushed on heedlessly, like the pale shimmer of green showing at the melting edge of snowbanks. Spring didn't blush and stammer and hang back, asking for sunny guarantees. It simply came as it could, struggling against winter's elemental grasp.

Dawn looked out the window and saw a moonlit land glittering whitely under a mantle of sleet and softer, equally sterile snow. It could have been November or February but for the dark patches showing beneath the snow, shadowy promises where the sun had nearly melted through to the seeds waiting within frigid ground.

A desperate need to go to the loom came to Dawn, a need to lose herself in creative rhythms and vivid colors, to see her dreams woven into a textured reality that enhanced rather than diminished the possibilities of life. But her loom might as well have been on a mountain peak for all its accessibility to her at that instant. She would die rather than walk back into Logan's bedroom uninvited.

With quiet, swift steps she went to the kitchen. The smell of spices and meat reminded her that she had made Colorado chili for the hands. She had promised to take it over to them that night, so that the dedicated chili hounds could have it for breakfast.

She had also promised some to Logan. Tonight.

Dawn took a slow, careful breath and put aside the panicky thought that she couldn't survive being Logan's mistress. It was like spring in the mountains. Too beautiful. Too cruel. But she had no choice except to bear it. For Logan's sake, and her own. She had to be strong enough to show him that love was more powerful than hate. Love was the sun, able to melt any winter, gentle any wild wind, draw life out of even the most frigid earth.

The spicy meat Dawn had left on the stove was tender, bubbling gently. She baked dozens of biscuits and wrapped them tightly against the cold. After reserving a portion of everything for Logan, she took a firm grip on the heavy, bubbling pot of chili and headed outside. The instant she set her foot onto the back porch step, Prowl appeared and rubbed against her shins with the unsubtle enthusiasm of a hungry cat.

"Running out of mice?" asked Dawn dryly.

Prowl yowled and stropped her sinuous lean length across Dawn's shins again.

"Watch it, cat!" warned Dawn, stumbling on the dark, icy path. She clutched the kettle of chili more tightly. The pot holders she was using slipped. A searing pain scored across her wrist as it moved heavily against the cast iron. She went down on one knee, barely managing to hang on to the heavy kettle long enough to set it aside.

Logan saw her fall as he stood at the upstairs window watching the hail-glittering, windswept night. His heart lurched as Dawn staggered and went down to her knees. She doubled over the kettle as though in pain. He couldn't see clearly what had happened. Then he saw her hand sweep over a patch of snow and return quickly to her other wrist.

She burned herself, thought Logan.

His hands clenched against the window frame until his knuckles were pale beneath his tanned skin. He swore bitterly, enraged at his own stupidity in not preventing the accident. He knew that Dawn used that walkway between the kitchen and bunkhouse several times a day. He should have told Turk to keep it free of ice. Better yet, he should have told Turk to carry his own damned food from the kitchen to the bunkhouse. As for the cat—if it tripped Dawn again, Logan would skin it for a hatband.

Motionless, his hands doubled into fists, Logan watched for what seemed an eternity as Dawn knelt and held snow on her wrist, dulling the unexpected, savage pain. Finally she stood, put the biscuits on top of the kettle again, picked up the chili pot and walked cautiously toward the bunkhouse. On the way back to the kitchen she swept up another handful of snow and held it against her wrist.

If you get any clumsier, she told herself bitterly, *Logan will need another nurse.*

And another mistress?

The question burned Dawn as surely as the kettle had. Love was irreplaceable. Mistresses were interchangeable.

Listen, klutz, she advised herself, holding snow against her burn, *you should be grateful that Logan wants vengeance as well as sex. It's the only thing that sets you apart from the other women he's had in his bed.*

The thought was as comforting as the winter wind scouring down from the peaks. Dawn shivered and went back into the house. The aroma of chili was incredibly rich after the empty, icy wind. Even so, her appetite didn't stir. The idea of eating was like the idea of lifting her Volkswagen and tucking it under her arm. Impossible. She began to fix a small tray for Logan, smoothing out a place mat she had woven. Its amber and gold colors were set off by accents of brown so dark they were almost black. Against the bleak winter night pouring through the windows, the weaving was like a swath of sleeping fire.

Dawn looked from the icy black of night to the pooled incandescence of the fabric and back again, realizing that they were part of a continuous design, that the sun's returning strength was all the more blessed for the icy darkness of winter. Without winter, spring's tentative warmth was unappreciated. Without darkness, light was commonplace. Without turmoil, peace was just another name for boredom.

The most beautiful patterns invariably sprang from the most difficult beginnings.

Dawn finished setting Logan's tray and carried it up to his room. She knocked lightly. There was no answer. Balancing the tray, she opened the door. Her breath came in sharply when she saw that the bed was empty. Logan was standing naked in front of the window, staring out at the bleak landscape as though it were a mirror. Dawn started to tell him that he shouldn't be up, but the words died on her lips as he turned around. She hadn't seen him naked before. Not all of him. Not like this.

Logan's amber eyes flicked from the clothes Dawn had abandoned on the floor to the clothes she wore now. She looked as though nothing had ever happened between them. Her hair was combed and tightly bound, as controlled as her expression. It angered him suddenly that his hunger was as hot and hard as ever and she was so serene, untouched.

"I liked you better naked and begging for me," he said.

He saw the flush that climbed her cheeks and the trembling of her hands as they tightened on the tray. He waited almost curiously to see whether she would lash out at him, and in doing so shatter her maddening serenity.

Wordlessly Dawn walked to the bed side and put down the tray. She didn't look at Logan again.

"Where's yours?" he asked, seeing that there was only one plate stacked on the tray.

"I'm not hungry," she said quietly, turning away.

Logan's hand shot out and closed around Dawn's arm. "Running away?" he asked lazily, pulling her close. He couldn't help the shudder that ran over him as his aroused, aggressive flesh bumped against her. "You've got a lot to learn about being a mistress. If I want you to strip naked and have a midnight snack with me, you'll do just that."

"I was going to get your coffee," she said tightly.

"Good. Bring it to me. Naked. With your hair loose."

Dawn closed her eyes. "Why?" she asked, her voice ragged. "More revenge?"

"I didn't know that being naked with me was so unpleasant," he said roughly, pushing away from her.

"That's not what I meant," Dawn said, feeling her control slipping away, leaving her as naked as he was. "Anger isn't the same as desire. You were angry with me when I walked into the room. You don't want me, Logan. You just want to—to parade your power over me."

"That's what being a mistress is all about," he retorted. "Not having power. You've got a lot to learn about how men and women treat each other. It's screw or be screwed. And let me tell you something," he added sardonically. "Any screwing that gets done around here gets done by me, not by Mary Sue's daughter."

"Mary Sue's daughter," Dawn repeated, feeling more of the pattern condense around her, a design as cold and enduring as winter itself. "That's really all you see when you look at me, isn't it? Mary Sue."

"I'd be a damned fool if I saw anything else," said Logan savagely, knowing even as he spoke that he was just that. A damned fool. He kept looking at Dawn and remembering her own blood on his body; yet her passionate response to him had been as untamed as fire, hotter, far more beautiful. She had given herself to him and then had wept at the sheer beauty of experiencing him inside her. "Forget the coffee," he said huskily, unbuttoning her blouse.

"Logan—" She looked at him but saw none of the contempt that had drawn his face into hard lines. She didn't understand the pattern of his shifts from ice to warmth and back again; she only knew that when he was like this, honest in his hunger for her, she couldn't refuse him.

"Don't argue, darling," he said, amusement curling beneath his voice as he unsnapped her bra and took her rosy nipple into his mouth. "It won't do any good. See?"

His teeth scraped lightly, skillfully across the tightening crown. She made a small sound of surprise and passion and held onto him as desire swept through her, making her dizzy. He felt the sudden shivering of her body and knew a fierce triumph that he had called such a response from her. She might look as cool as a spring glacier, but she couldn't resist the desire he aroused in her any more than he could resist the idea of being tightly sheathed within her satin heat again.

Logan felt Dawn's hands tangle in his hair as he undressed her. She flinched and hesitated for an instant as he pulled off her blouse. He remembered that she had hurt herself. Gently he turned her right wrist up so that he could see it. A dark red welt spread angrily across her skin. The contrast between the burn and the porcelain smoothness of her inner arm made Logan angry at himself all over again.

With exquisite gentleness he brushed his lips against her unburned skin.

"No more carrying hot kettles over icy paths for you," he said almost harshly. "Does it hurt?"

The concern beneath Logan's rough voice made Dawn catch her breath, as did the softness of his mouth caressing her skin. "I don't know," she said honestly.

"What?" he asked, watching her with eyes the color and clarity of cognac.

"I don't know if it hurts." Dawn's fingers threaded into Logan's thick hair, hungrily seeking his warmth. "When you touch me," she said softly, "that's all I can feel. You. Touching me."

A shudder ripped through Logan's powerful body. He bent and took Dawn's mouth in a kiss that didn't end until she was naked and he was inside her and their shared ecstasy made the idea of pain impossible.

This time he fell asleep holding her, tightly locked within her warmth and the seductive peace that she wove around him.

Ten

April sunlight poured through the upstairs window, gentled by the golden shimmer of the curtain Dawn had made. Although a cold front had been predicted, there was no sign of it yet. It was a glorious day that fairly shouted of life returning to the frozen land.

Logan moved impatiently in the bed, feeling as irritabl as a bear with a broken tooth. There was too much to do o the ranch for him to put up with lying around any longer The only thing that had kept him in bed even part-time wa Dawn. In addition to his unending hunger for her passion he had discovered a decided weakness for having her cool his food and rub his back and pamper him in general. In th afternoons when his fever sometimes returned, it was ver pleasant to lie in bed and watch her weave, and then to fal asleep to the ancient rhythms of loom and shuttle.

She's addictive, you stupid son of a bitch, Logan tol himself savagely. *She's weaving herself into your life a surely as she weaves colors into that tapestry she's making*

But it's on my terms, he reminded himself. *She's my mistress, not my lover or my fiancée. She never refuses me in bed. Never. I'm not her toy. She's mine! When I get tired of her I'll say goodbye and that will be the end of it.*

What Logan tried not to think about was the fact that he wanted Dawn more, not less, with each day. If he hadn't been sure that he was in control of her sensual response, his need for her would have appalled him. Even so, he found himself reminding her of her mistress status more and more often, and then disliking himself for the flash of hurt she could not quite conceal. Slowly, almost invisibly, day by day, hour by hour, cut by cut, she was retreating from him.

But not in bed. Never in bed.

Hurt or be hurt. Screw or be screwed. You made your choice a long time ago, he reminded himself coldly. *Would you rather end up like Joe?*

There was no answer to that. There never had been. Broodingly Logan watched Dawn's slender fingers work over the loom. She didn't notice his attention. She was basking in the April sun glowing through the upstairs window. In the days since the hailstorm, the weather had been beautiful—warm, clear, sunlight flowing like an endless golden tide over the land. At the ranch's elevation, snow remained only on the northern slopes, in the forests and in the deepest ravines. White-faced cows moved heavily over the ground as they searched out the first tender green shoots. Soon calves would be born and the pastures would echo with the cries of new life.

With an unconscious sigh Dawn looked away from the window. She wanted to go outside for just a little while before the weather changed back to winter, to hold out her hands to the warm rush of spring and smell the sweet wind as it poured over her. But the only thing keeping Logan in bed was her presence; he enjoyed watching her weave even when he was in a foul mood. And his mood today was just that. Foul. She knew it even though he had barely spoken two words.

Dawn also knew that Logan would get up and pace like a caged cat as soon as she left the room. Dr. Martin had told Logan that he should wait another week before resuming any part of his workload. Logan had argued rather violently before giving in. When he had finally agreed, it was with a cutting remark about how getting a clean bill of health was the only way he could get rid of his nurse. The words had hurt Dawn but they hadn't surprised her.

It was part of the pattern that was growing between her and Logan. Though he could not hide his desire for her, he made sure that she never forgot she was in his bed because she was his mistress, not his lover. He came to her, made her cry out with need and fulfillment, fell asleep holding her—and then he would turn around in the morning and scorn her. He would admit only to wanting her body, not her love. In spite of that, he made love to her with exquisite care, showing an intensity and naked need that never failed to move her.

And afterward he cut her to the bone, needing to prove that he felt nothing at all for her but lust.

Understanding Logan's pattern didn't keep Dawn from being hurt each time he turned on her. Nor did it give her hope for the future. The greater the intimacy of the lovemaking or the shared, sweet silences, the deeper the wounding that inevitably followed. Nothing she did softened Logan or deflected his anger.

At times she was afraid that he truly hated her.

That fear had grown in Dawn until it was like a black, cold night absorbing the tentative fire of spring. The closer she came to Logan the harder he pushed her away. Even the rocks high in the peaks couldn't survive wild alternations between fire and ice without breaking. She loved him—and she was afraid that she was breaking. She found herself retreating more and more into her weaving, offering only the most neutral kind of conversation, rarely catching his eye, rarely smiling, always trying to do nothing that would call down his icy rage on her.

Sometimes she believed that his revenge wouldn't be complete until he broke her. Then it wasn't fear she felt. It was despair.

Common sense told Dawn to leave. Love and hope told her to stay, that Logan needed her, that something beautiful and enduring could be created out of the destructive pattern of the past. She had given her word to be his mistress as long as he wanted her. It had been the only way to prove to him that she wasn't like Mary Sue, a woman who promised everything and gave nothing at all.

It can't be just revenge Logan wants from me, Dawn reassured herself fiercely. *No man who hated me could touch me like Logan does, with so much tenderness and a passion that shakes both of us. Surely he must care for me, if only a little.*

But words were just words. Patterns were different. Patterns were real. And this pattern became more bleak with each repetition, each rejection, until it was a darkness that was relieved by only a few incandescent threads woven through, hinting at future designs that might be rich with colors and possibilities.

With another unconscious sigh, Dawn continued weaving. The shuttle flew from side to side, paused, and then came the rhythmic thumping as she packed the newly woven weft into place. When she was finished, the warp was invisible. Beneath her flying fingers a tide of iridescent indigo-black arose, as though night were alive and coldly seething within the confines of the loom. Randomly, like sparks, came tiny flashes of scarlet or gold that had been born out of the many shades of darkness. The sketch hanging beside the loom showed how the sparks would ultimately unite into a fiery sunrise of life, becoming flames intertwined into two figures that could have been lovers.

Logan's eyes went from the sketch to the loom where darkness seethed. The sparks of color were very brief, all but overwhelmed by the woven layers of icy midnight. He didn't see how the design was going to work. It looked so much darker on the loom than it did in the sketch.

"Do your designs always work?" he asked.

Dawn flinched as though she had been struck. Logan frowned, seeing it as one more sign of how she had been drifting away from him. She never came to him with a smile or an offer of conversation as she had before she became his mistress. Whenever she wasn't actually in bed with him she was either cooking downstairs, taking care of the cowhands, or lost in her weaving.

So what if she doesn't want to talk? he asked himself impatiently. *She never refuses me in bed.*

That had surprised him. He had been cold and cutting to her, goading her, trying to make her refuse him so he could point out that she was just like her mother. A tease. But Dawn hadn't refused him, hadn't teased him. She simply…went away…somewhere inside herself after he lashed out. She didn't argue with him anymore about Joe or anything else. Logan's food was fresh and hot. His clothes were clean. When he wanted her body all he had to do was reach out and take it. The only emotion she showed was when he was deep inside her. Then all that she had hidden came tumbling out, the words and the cries and the heat of her.

Logan realized that Dawn hadn't answered his question. "Do they always work?" he repeated.

"Most of the time," she said quietly, not looking up as she used what looked like a giant wooden sword to pack down the weft.

"What about the ones that don't?"

She shrugged and didn't answer.

"Do you have to finish them before you know they won't work?" persisted Logan.

"No."

"Then when do you know? Halfway through? Sooner? Later?"

Harnesses shifted, opening a new shed for the shuttle to pass through.

"Yes," she said finally.

"Yes what?"

"Just yes. Halfway. Sooner. Later. Each pattern is different."

"How?"

Dawn looked at the dark design, then at the sketch. She picked out a few strings of warp by hand, and wove in a single short strand of metallic gold. She tamped it into place with a small wooden comb and resumed weaving on the darker body of the work.

"How do you know which designs to give up on, and when?" asked Logan.

She heard his impatience and braced herself for another round of coldness and withdrawal. This morning when they had awakened he had made love to her so beautifully that she had cried helplessly and clung to him, unable even to tell him why. He had held her, comforted her, given her peace, acted as though he cared for her.

And now he would destroy that peace, deny that caring, proving in icy sentences that she was nothing more than a sexual convenience to him. That was his pattern. She had been expecting his cruelty all morning. She had tried to avoid it by avoding talking with him. It hadn't worked.

She wondered if anything would, if vengeance was simply too strong, too compelling for love to overcome.

"It depends on how well I like the design," she said in a voice that was as neutral and unprovocative as she knew how to make it. "The better I like the pattern, the longer I work before I admit defeat."

"What about my pattern?" asked Logan, watching Dawn intently, his amber eyes narrowed.

Dawn gave him a startled look before she realized that he was referring to the tapestry she was making for him, the one she was supposed to weave strands of her own hair into, making the flame-lovers cast a shimmering shadow.

"What about it?" she asked, packing down the weft with short, hard strokes.

"Would you give up on my pattern halfway through? Sooner? Later?"

The harnesses shifted rhythmically, quickly. Dawn reached for another shuttle, one on which the yarn was more blue than black.

"It's not for me to give up," she said.

"What?"

"As you said, it's your pattern. I'll work on it until you tell me to leave. That was our bargain."

"I wasn't talking about you being my mistress," said Logan harshly, angry without knowing why.

"Weren't you?" Then, she continued quickly, "The design has many beautiful possibilities. I wouldn't give up until I'd tried each one and had each fail."

"What do you do with the tapestries that don't work?" he asked, goaded by the absolute emotional neutrality of Dawn's voice. "Unravel them?"

The loom's pulsing heart missed a beat before resuming. Dawn realized that Logan wasn't going to let her evade a fight with him.

So be it, she thought with a calm that was just short of numbness and despair. *Then we'll fight over something that matters, something that has even the tiniest chance of altering the pattern of destruction.*

"No," she said softly. "I don't unravel a bad design. I cut it from the loom and burn it to ash."

The words went through Logan like an icy rain, telling him more than he wanted to hear.

"You see," Dawn continued, her voice calm, precise, as relentless as the beat of weaver's sword and harnesses shifting as she worked. "The point of mistakes is to learn exactly as much as they have to teach you—no more, no less—and then to walk away and never look back. When I fail at weaving, the lesson I learn is not that I should give up the loom. I learn that I should be more careful in selecting future designs.

"That was your mistake, Logan," she said, continuing to weave swiftly, numbly. "You learned more from the past than it had to teach. You learned that women are cruel teases who will destroy men who love. So you stopped loving. That's like me refusing to weave because of one failed design. I don't. I simply learn to make better patterns. Failure isn't an end. It's a beginning. Unless, of course, you wallow in it rather than learn from it."

"I told you not to bring up Joe again," Logan said softly, dangerously.

"I haven't. But the shoe fits so well, doesn't it? Except it's not your own failed pattern you're caught in. It's his."

"Damn you!" Logan grated, sitting up in a powerful surge. "What gives you the right to tell me how to live?"

Dawn's hands trembled. Carefully she laid down the long weaver's sword she had just used to pack the weft into place. "I'm not telling you how to live," she said with a desperate calm. "I'm trying to point out the pattern of your life, because you're hurting yourself so badly with it. You won't let yourself trust a woman because you don't want to be like your brother. Helpless. All women aren't like Mary Sue. All men aren't like your brother. But you don't want to believe that, because then you'll have to face what your brother was—and what he wasn't. He wasn't strong, Logan. You are.''

"That's enough!"

"No," said Dawn, fighting against the tears closing her throat. "Not quite. Rather than learn from the past you'll destroy the present. Like your brother. He couldn't forget, forgive or get revenge on Mary Sue. You could get vengeance, though. You did. But taking away the Lazy W wasn't enough. Now you're destroying me, even though I'm not like my mother at all. What is my crime, Logan? Your brother hated Mary Sue because she never gave herself to him. Yet the more I give myself to you, the more you hate me. Why?"

"Do you think I'd sleep with a woman I hated?" he asked, his voice savage.

"Yes," Dawn said starkly. "For revenge. If you thought you could make her love you—and then destroy her! Your brother's dead and my mother is beyond your reach. But I'm not, and you know that I loved you three years ago. And—" Dawn's voice broke, then resumed again "—I look just like Mary Sue. That's all you see when you look at me. Hatred. Revenge. My mother."

Logan said nothing, simply watched Dawn with predatory amber eyes.

She tilted back her head and closed her eyes, trying to prevent tears from falling. "Don't you see the pattern? Every time we give each other any warmth, any peace, any pleasure, you turn and claw me. The closer we come, the worse the clawing. Like now. It was so beautiful with you this morning. And ever since I left your arms I've been waiting to be punished. I've been waiting to be cut by you until I bleed."

She didn't hear Logan take a sharp breath or see the sudden tightening of his body. "If—" She bit her lip for a long moment and then continued. "If I thought it were doing you

any good, I'd endure it somehow. But it isn't. The more revenge you get, the more you want. You're destroying yourself as well as me. There's no pattern but destruction, no
chance—"

Dawn turned and looked at Logan out of eyes the color
of spring, but her voice was as bleak as January. "Mary Sue
could take this. I can't. I am not my mother. I can't live with
cruelty like this and survive. I don't think you can, either.
Let me go, Logan. If you care anything at all for yourself or
me, *let me go.*"

"No." The word was quick, final. Then he added coldly,
"Going to run again, Dawn? I never expected you to keep
your word to me, but what about your debt to Kathy? Or
did Dr. Martin give me a clean bill of health yesterday?"

Dawn's eyes closed and every line of her body showed
defeat. Dr. Martin had told her privately that Logan was all
but recovered, yet it would be better if he took another week
of "easy living." That way there would be no chance of another relapse. If she left, there would be no one to keep Logan from falling back into his old pattern of working
himself into the ground to avoid the empty nights.

Silently Dawn picked up her shuttle and began to weave
another color of darkness into Logan's pattern. He
watched, seething with unreleased anger, wondering why he
didn't feel triumphant. Joe would have sold his soul to have
this kind of control over Mary Sue, to be able to reach into
her and make her bleed.

*That's just what you're doing. Selling your soul. And
Dawn's.*

Logan rejected the thought the instant it came. With a
restless movement he snatched the latest issue of a stock-
man's magazine from the bedside table and began to read.
The muted rhythms of the loom wove through the silence.
After he had read several articles, the rhythmic sounds

stopped. He looked up in time to see Dawn leaving the loom.

"Where are you going?" Logan's voice sounded hard and suspicious, even to himself. He grimaced at the sound, making his expression even more fierce. He had never questioned her before. It was different now; he knew at some primitive level that he was pushing her too hard. He expected her to run.

She has to run. She's too close. I'm too weak. When I cut her I bleed, too. It has to end before she finds out that I'm as helpless as Joe.

Yet Logan didn't want Dawn to leave. Just watching her walk made him hungry. He wanted to hold her, drink in her soft cries, watch her while she slept in his arms. He wanted—too much. Too close. Tangled in her softness and peace.

"There's wash to do," she said, her voice like her skin, pale. "Bread to make. A bunkhouse to clean."

A stranger's voice. Logan compared the toneless neutrality with the subdued music that he had come to expect from Dawn. He frowned again.

"How long do you usually sulk?" he asked coolly, angry at himself for noticing, for caring, for wanting to hear the music again.

His only answer was the soft closing of the bedroom door behind her. He picked up the magazine again, opened it and threw it aside with a curse. He picked up the tray containing all the ranch bills and receipts. Swearing beneath his breath, he began to bring the accounts up to date. By the time he looked up again it was nearly noon. He frowned at the bedside clock.

Where is she?

His temper uncurled like a whip as he realized that he had been asking that question more and more frequently in the past week. Dawn would get up from her weaving and be gone for half an hour or an hour, sometimes even longer. She never said where she was going or what she was doing. Sometimes he could hear her moving around downstairs, working on the small loom she used to make bright place mats and napkins for him. Sometimes he heard her in the kitchen, and then would come tantalizing scents of fresh bread and cookies, roasts and potatoes and tender fruit pies. If it was the wash she was doing, she would come upstairs with arm loads of fresh clothes. She would put them on the bed and talk to him while she folded them.

And then he would unravel her silky braid and take the clothes from her creamy body, sinking into her, wrapping her around him; and he would want to shout and weep with the ecstasy he found in her sweet flesh. Just the thought of it was enough and more than enough to make him swell with a hunger that grew greater each time he took what she so generously gave. Herself.

And what are you giving her in return? part of Logan's mind asked sardonically. *Kind words? Money? Security?*

She hasn't complained until a few hours ago, he retorted to himself.

People paying debts don't complain. Lovers complain. And women in love complain. Guess she's not in love with you anymore, huh?

I don't want her love—just her body.

Keep telling yourself that, cowboy. One day you might wake up dumb enough to believe it.

Logan got out of bed, yanked on his clothes and stalked out of the bedroom. If he stayed upstairs arguing with himself any longer he would start kicking down the walls.

Even though clouds from the new storm front were already gathering, it was still sunny outside, tantalizing, and the air was soft with promises of an enduring thaw. He was damned if he was going to play sick any longer just to keep

Dawn on a short leash. He had been up and about every instant when she was out of the room. He didn't have his full power back, but he was stronger physically than he had been since summer. He was more than capable of getting on a horse and riding to check on the cattle.

Maybe if I get back to work I won't want Dawn so much. I've been bored and she's been there. That's all there is to it. Nothing surprising, really. I itched and she scratched. Happens all the time.

Logan crossed the yard and went toward the barn. Sand gritted beneath his feet as he walked on the stone pathway. he smiled grimly. Turk had kept the walkway all but buried in sand since Logan had torn a strip off him for letting it get icy in the first place. Logan's smile faded as he thought of the scarf that Dawn had given to the broad-shouldered cowhand. If she hadn't woven one for Shorty, too, Logan would have raised hell. As it was, he couldn't even complain without looking like a jealous fool.

Nonetheless it rankled every time Logan thought of Turk wearing something woven by Dawn's gentle hands.

The sound of her laughter coming out of the bunkhouse stopped Logan like a blow. Without thinking, he spun around and walked quickly to the bunkhouse door. It was open, as were all the windows.

The first thing he saw was Dawn.

She had unbuttoned the top buttons of her cardigan sweater and pushed up her sleeves above the elbow. She was bent over the bed, stripping it of covers with graceful motions. Her hair was woven into a French braid that came only as far as her neck. From there, silky black strands fanned out over her back and shoulders and fell like ribbons of black silk over the sheets. Her jeans fit her body as snugly as Logan did when he made love to her. She had a rosy flush on her cheeks and her eyes were the vivid green of an aspen's first tender buds.

Logan heard a rumble of male speech. Dawn threw back her head and laughed. The sound was so beautiful that it froze him where he stood. Motionless, aching, he drank the sweetness of Dawn's laughter.

Why doesn't she laugh like that with me?

The question—and its obvious answer—made Logan angry. He strode into the bunkhouse. No one noticed. Turk was handing Dawn a pillowcase that he had just peeled from his pillow. He was laughing down at her, his hat swept back to reveal the thickly curling hair, his black eyes dancing with amusement. And she was laughing, too, watching Turk as though she had never seen a man quite so interesting.

"Turk, you ought to be ashamed of yourself, telling a joke like that to Miz Sheridan," chided Shorty from the small bunkhouse kitchen where he was slamming pans around. Despite his half-serious complaint, his voice was struggling against laughter.

Turk made a sound of disgust. "Hell, Lily told me the joke yesterday."

"But Lily's a—"

Turk turned suddenly on Shorty. "Watch it, old man."

Shorty flushed. "She's different from Miz Sheridan," he insisted stubbornly.

"How?" asked Logan's icy voice from the doorway. "They're both sleeping with men who have no intention of marrying them." He looked toward Dawn, his face hard with anger and contempt. The need to fight that had been riding him since he had made love to her that morning had finally found its release. "You've got a short memory," he said to Dawn. "I told you what I'd do if you so much as looked at another man."

Dawn was too shocked by Logan's words and by the contempt on his face to move. "I wasn't—"

"Like hell you weren't," he interrupted roughly. "Is this what you've been doing while I was getting well? Sneaking out to the bunkhouse for a quickie with God's gift to the local ladies?''

"You're crazy," said Turk flatly. "She's never so much as looked sideways at me or any man the whole time she's been here. And it's not because we wouldn't look back! The way you treat her you're lucky she—"

Logan looked at Turk. Just looked. Turk jerked back with the automatic reflex of a man who has felt the ground give way beneath his feet. The violence seething within Logan was almost tangible, needing only an outlet to become all too real. Shorty took one look and slid out the back door. He had seen enough of Logan's temper in the past few years to know that anyone who stuck around now was either a fool or crazy.

"Get back to work," said Logan. "If I catch you near her again you'll leave the ranch in pieces. Hear me?"

Turk hesitated, nodded curtly and left the bunkhouse.

"You," continued Logan, turning on Dawn, "have two minutes to get undressed and lie down on that mattress."

Dawn's face went white. A hot tide of humiliation crawled up her body. "Why are you doing this?" she whispered.

"Doing what?" he asked, unsnapping his shirt with a swift ripping motion.

"Treating me like this."

"How else should I treat a cheating little whore?"

"Logan, I didn't do anything! You know I didn't!"

"His eyes were eating you and you were loving every second of it. You laughed."

"He told a joke. That's all, Logan. Just a joke."

"Guess who's going to get the last laugh?" he retorted, grabbing her arm.

With swift, efficient motions he yanked open her sweater and jerked it off her arms. Her bra went next, carelessly discarded on the floor. His hands moved over her roughly, almost bruisingly, making her flinch away. With a curse he jerked her close. One hand tangled in her hair, forcing her head back. Hard fingers fastened on her breast, demanding a response. She inhaled sharply, but it was fear rather than passion that made her eyes dark.

"Don't do this to me, Logan," she whispered.

"You're my mistress. I'll do whatever I like, whenever I like, wherever I like. Got that?" he said, looking down at her with eyes that were narrowed, bleak. "Mistress. Not my girlfriend. Not my lover. Not my woman. Just plain mistress."

Dawn made a choked sound and covered her ears, unable to retreat for the hard arm holding her pinned to his side. He yanked her hands away and bent down to her.

"Understand now?" he snarled. "Do you finally understand what you are to me?"

"Yes!" she cried, struggling futilely to escape him.

"Good. Now lie down."

"No."

"What did you say?" he asked softly.

Dawn closed her eyes, unable to look any longer at the bleak, cruel face of the man she had been fool enough to love.

"No!"

"You can't refuse me," he said, his voice cold and final.

The rage that had been building in Logan exploded, burning through his inner arguments, his doubts, leaving only the certainty that he must be the one who controlled their relationship. With frightening ease he took her down onto the bare mattress.

Dawn struggled until she was exhausted, but she was overmatched. She had always been overmatched with Logan. Her love. His hate. Her desire to heal. His desire for vengeance. Her need to create. His need to destroy.

Nothing she had done had made any difference.

Despair closed around Dawn. She shut her eyes and turned her head aside, no longer seeing Logan's body looming over her or feeling his touch. With every bit of control she had, she retreated in the only way left to her. Into herself. She sought oblivion with every part of her mind and body, withdrawing further and further, letting light drain out of the world. A blessed kind of numbness stole over her, a feeling of unreality. She wasn't really there. She was somewhere else. Somewhere no one could reach her.

And it was cold there, as cold and bleak as the past.

Logan felt the change in Dawn. There was nothing in his arms but dead weight and the shocking coldness of her flesh. As he looked at her lifeless face he realized what he had almost done. His hand fell away from her jeans and his face went as white as hers. Very gently he rolled aside, pulling her with him, trying to warm both of them. There was still no response. He spoke her name softly, repeatedly, because it was the only word that came to him in his need.

The voice calling Dawn's name was hoarse, but it was concern rather than anger that gave the roughness. And the hands stroking her moved with gentleness where before there had been only rage. Slowly she opened her eyes. Logan was watching her, his face taut with emotion. She tried to speak but no words came. He bent and brushed his lips over hers as gently as sunshine touching the first flowers of spring.

Very carefully Logan released Dawn. He bent down, picked up her sweater and covered her with hands that shook. He found his discarded shirt and put it on, fumbling over the snaps. As Dawn watched, she realized that somehow Logan had gotten control of his destructive rage. He hadn't forced her despite the hunger that she could see thrusting rigidly against his worn jeans. In the end lust hadn't been strong enough, hatred hadn't been strong enough, rage hadn't been strong enough, even the pattern of the past hadn't been strong enough to make Logan destroy her, and himself.

"Logan," she said huskily.

He closed his eyes and a shudder moved visibly through his powerful body. "Don't. I want you too much. Don't you understand? When I look at you all I can think of is being inside you, hearing your cries against my throat, knowing that I'm giving you a pleasure no man ever has. I can't force you, *yet I have to have you.*"

Logan opened his eyes and stared down at Dawn. She wanted to cry out at the pain she saw there. She ached to hold him, to comfort him, to warm both of them in the love she had for him.

"You were right," he said bleakly. "I should let you go. But I can't. I can promise you one thing, though." He gestured roughly toward the bed. "I'll cut off my hands before I let that happen again."

He turned and left the bunkhouse, moving swiftly, afraid that if he looked at her any longer he would be lost.

Eleven

Dawn sat in the empty room, holding her grandmother's spindle in one hand. In the other she held a few separate strands of her own long hair. As she spun the spindle's smooth golden wood, she deftly twisted long strands of hair into a single slender yarn. The result was both darkness and translucence, as though the yarn was illuminated from within. Absently she pulled another hair from the mass that rippled down her back in a sleek black fall. The new piece of hair was caught up with the old on the spindle's swiftly turning body. The yarn grew almost magically beneath her fingers in a technique that had been old thousands of years before man first scratched enigmatic marks on clay tablets.

A buffeting wind shook the ranch house as Dawn measured the length of the yarn she had created, nodded to herself and went to the tapestry. It was two-thirds done. The tones and textures of yellow and orange had spiraled out of darkness. At the center of the leaping fire, two flame-figures were intertwined in a graceful embrace. Dawn wove the unique shimmering yarn she had just made through the tapestry, using a darning needle. The figures slowly became both more distinct and more elusive, creatures of luminous shadow and shimmering light.

The wind blew around the ranch house in a low, sustained moan. Dawn didn't look up from the tapestry. Only one sound would have reached through her concentration, and it was a sound she didn't expect to hear—Logan's voice calling her name. In the five days since he had left her in the bunkhouse, he had spoken to her only when necessary and had touched her not at all. She no longer spent the nights locked in his arms or awakened to the feel of his body curved warmly along hers. He no longer first seduced and then rejected her. He barely noticed her at all. He vanished out into the ranch's cold, windswept valley for a work day that stretched from dawn to dusk and beyond. At her insistence Dr. Martin had come to the Lazy W, declared Logan sound of body and soft of mind, and left.

Sometimes Dawn thought she should have left with the doctor; but Logan hadn't released her from her word. He wouldn't touch her, but she was still his until he told her she could go. She knew that he still wanted her. It was there in his eyes every time she turned and found him watching her with a need that made her heart turn over. When she had suggested that he would be more comfortable without her, he had simply stared at her and said, "It's a little late for you to be thinking of that, isn't it?"

The only time the grim lines of his face had lightened at all was when Kathy's husband had called and announced that Logan was now the proud uncle of two healthy, identical baby girls. Dawn would never forget Logan's sudden smile, nor the love and gentleness and warmth that lit his amber eyes as he talked to Kathy on the phone. Dawn didn't know that her own eyes reflected her raw hunger for his love until Logan turned and saw her watching him. For an instant he looked as though he had been struck from behind—surprise and pain mingled. Then Kathy's words had claimed his attention again and the moment passed, leaving Dawn even more lonely than before.

Dawn straightened slowly from the tapestry, stretching her back. Absently she glanced out the bedroom window. What she saw caused her hands to go utterly still. Reflexively she fixed the needle to the tapestry before she went to stand at the window. Cold reached out to her through the double-paned glass. The storm front that had been predicted had arrived on schedule and refused to leave. A foot of new snow cloaked the high peaks and choked the narrow valleys feeding into the broad valley that was the heart of the Lazy W.

And now the wind was taking that new powdery snow and stripping it from exposed slopes, sending veils of ice crystals scudding knee-high along the contours of the land. Dawn knew by the cold radiating through the glass that it was below freezing outside. With the windchill factor it would be below zero. But that wasn't what held her motionless, staring out over the valley. It was the sight of a cow leaving the herd and drifting off on a tangent.

Only one thing would send a cow off alone in such weather. Like most herd animals, cows calved by themselves. As Dawn looked, she saw other cows scattered away from the herd, cows hunched like small russet boulders against the blowing snow and barren earth. Riders moved among the cattle, searching for newly born calves.

"No," whispered Dawn. "Not now."

Abruptly she turned away from the window. No matter when the range cows were bred, it seemed that they all calved at once. Logan would need every rider he could get to keep the cows from losing the newborn calves to the brutal cold.

There was no hesitation in Dawn, no need to consider what had to be done. She had been raised on the Lazy W. She knew where the cows would hide from a northern wind and where they went to calve in secret. Within minutes she was running downstairs, dressed in thermal underwear and layers of wool. She pulled on a scarlet ski parka and pants. When she yanked her knit mask into place, nothing but her eyes were unprotected.

She ran to the corral, hoping that no one had taken Bigfoot, the huge bay gelding she had trained years ago, when the Lazy W and everything on it belonged to the Sheridan rather than to the Garrett family. Bigfoot had a nose like a hound when it came to sniffing out cattle. It wouldn't be the first time she had ridden him through snow in search of newborn calves.

Bigfoot was still in the main corral, his rump to the wind and his head low. He humped his back at the cold saddle but turned into the wind without argument. Dawn rode quickly into the main pasture where the pregnant cows were being held. The pasture was the valley itself, a long swath of rumpled land that would have to be searched and then searched again as cows followed their instinct to hide and give birth alone.

Icy grass crunched beneath Bigfoot's hooves. Some of the frozen grass was brown, the legacy of last summer's bounty. Some was the same tender green as the lilac bushes coming into bud between the main corral and the barn. Against the bleak winter colors of the valley, Dawn's scarlet stood out like a shout. A rider who had been circling the main herd broke away and cantered toward her. The man adjusted effortlessly to every change in the big buckskin's gait. Dawn watched and felt longing twist through her more painfully than any ice-tipped wind.

"What the hell do you think you're doing?" Logan demanded.

"Did you think I'd stay inside while calves were dying in this cold?" she asked evenly.

"Not your ranch. Not your calves. Not your problem. Go back to the house."

She shivered, but it wasn't the wind. It was the coldness of him, worse than before. Each day. Worse.

"I know this ranch as well as any hand here." She reached out suddenly, gripping Logan's wrist. "Please. The calves are so small, so helpless in the first hours."

Logan looked at the wide green eyes surrounded by the black knit mask and felt unwanted emotions tearing through him. He knew what it would be like if the wind blew through the night. Brutal was the kindest word he could think of to describe it. He didn't want her out there, breaking her heart over something she couldn't change. *So small, so helpless.*

"You're riding with me," he said, his voice as hard as his eyes. "If you get out of my sight, I will personally tie you up and throw you in the truck with the calves. Hear me?"

"I hear," she said, removing her hand. As he started to rein his horse around she added softly, "Thank you."

Logan's body stiffened. His hands flexed into fists. "For what?" he asked harshly. "Giving you a ticket to hell?"

He looked unreasonably big in his sheepskin riding coat and chaps. Snow whitened the outer surface of his clothes. The only bit of color on him was the long scarlet and gold scarf that Dawn had woven for him. His eyes were dark, haunted, and his face was drawn taut. She knew that he shouldn't have been working for the past five days. The knowledge that her presence had driven him from the house was more painful to her than the ice-sharpened wind. Without stopping to think she leaned forward and pulled his scarf into place, protecting his face from the frigid wind. He flinched from her touch in the instant before he spun the buckskin on its hocks and headed back across the pasture.

In the lee of the wind, snow had piled into drifts that were belly high to a tall horse. Logan's buckskin broke trail. Bigfoot followed. Both riders looked for any sign of cows that had sought shelter from the wind and a quiet place to give birth.

By the time they found the first calf, the sun had set behind veils of ice crystals thrown up by the vicious wind. Bigfoot had just passed downwind of a straggle of evergreens that looked too small to hide a cow, but the horse stopped, sniffed the air like a hound and tugged at the reins.

"Logan!" shouted Dawn, hoping he could hear over the rising howl of the wind.

The buckskin turned instantly. Dawn pointed toward the trees as she gave Bigfoot his head. Within minutes they had found the cow. One calf had been born and licked clean and was fighting to get to its feet. Each time it stood, the wind knocked the calf back down to the icy earth. Each time the calf was slower to struggle to its feet, weaker, colder. The cow wasn't able to help. She was on her side in the snow, giving birth to a second calf.

Dawn dismounted as Logan swooped up the first calf and turned his back to the wind, sheltering the struggling newborn from the icy blasts that swooped among the trees. Dawn knelt on the frigid ground just as the second calf was born. Even though every nerve screamed for her to snatch the calf from its frozen bed, she waited for the cow to stand and turn and lick her calf. Without those moments of intimate contact, the cow wouldn't recognize this calf as her own when the time came to reunite them.

"Hurry up!" said Dawn in an agonized voice as she saw the first shivers take the calf while its mother's tongue made a leisurely tour of the little body.

"That's long enough," called Logan. "We'll raise it by hand if we have to!"

The wind broke over them in an icy wave that bent the trees like grass. Dawn grabbed the calf and staggered to her feet. Calves were tiny only in comparison to cows. Thirty-five pounds of rather lively animal was a double armful for Dawn. Logan walked over and grabbed the calf under his free arm while Dawn mounted. He handed the calf up to her and helped her settle it across the front of her saddle. Then he mounted with the remaining calf tucked under one arm. The wind gusted, peeling an icy veil of snow from the land and flinging it up into their faces with a howl that drowned out the mama cow's bawls of distress as she followed the two horses to the fence.

The truck's headlights wore twin coronas of ice-hazed light. As Logan handed the twins over the fence, Dawn looked back over her shoulder. Even with the moon overhead, it was impossible to make out the black rise of the mountains across the half-mile wide neck of the pasture. She could feel the wind getting stronger. Man and animal alike had bits of ice and snow plastered over them. It wasn't a blizzard yet, but it was getting closer every minute. The thought made her want to cry out in protest. Finding calves in a full-scale blizzard would not only be dangerous, it would be impossible.

Dawn shivered and looked back at Logan.

"Take them to the heated stalls," Logan yelled to Shorty.

The truck retreated too quickly for the cow to follow. She stood disconsolately, head down, rump to the raging wind.

In the darkness it was all but impossible to spot solitary cows. Tracks were buried quickly in the open. As the wind and the night wore on, the riders were reduced to searching the ravines and meager windbreaks one foot at a time, crisscrossing the three-mile-long pasture repeatedly. More calves were born. Fewer were found. Of those that were, many were dead or dying.

Dawn began to dread the moment when her flashlight picked out the shape of a solitary cow, and the tiny mound of frozen snow-covered flesh that was her calf.

Cold became as much a part of Dawn as the shooting pains in her arms and back and legs. Staying in the saddle became harder and harder. She didn't know how long she had been out, for the moon was gone and the stars were lost to the icy gale. Her mind told her that it was barely past midnight. Her emotions said that she had been born in the cold saddle, lived there and would be buried there in winding sheets of ice. Twice Logan had told Dawn to go back to the house. She hadn't even bothered to refuse. She had simply lifted the reins and urged her horse to find one more calf. Just one.

Alive.

As the night ground on, a feeling of futility drained Dawn's strength as surely as the cold did. It had been a long time since any of the men had found a live calf. Hours. She knew that calves were being born around her in the darkness and howling wind. She knew that somehow most would survive on their own, a miraculous testament to the tenacity of life and renewal. She tried not to think of the calves that would not be lucky enough or strong enough. She had seen too many of them tonight—their tiny, perfect hooves and their curling eyelashes encased in ice. The last time she had been so close to finding the calf before it was killed by the cold. Just a few minutes sooner, just a few, just—

A ticket to hell.

Logan's words echoed in Dawn's mind like an epitaph for this unforgiving season. The thought of finding one more dead calf made her want to scream and cry and curse the endless, careless wind. She was driven by an unreasonable need to keep going despite the mental and physical exhaustion that made her body unresponsive to even the most simple commands. She would not let herself give up until she knew that somewhere, in some small way, she had woven a little warmth into the cold, savage pattern of this cruel spring.

Bigfoot lifted his head and turned into a patch of wind-scoured night that looked the same as every other piece of blackness. Dawn held her breath and prayed that it wouldn't be another dead calf that the horse had found. As soon as Bigfoot stopped she dismounted, only to go sprawling to her hands and knees as her cold body refused to take her weight. She thought she heard Logan calling her name but she ignored it and continued to dig frantically through a small mound of snow. She sensed him kneeling beside her, felt his hand on her arm as he tried to pull her away.

"Dawn—" His voice was as ragged as the wind.

"No!" she shouted frantically, shaking off his hand. "It's alive! I know it!"

Logan pulled the calf's unresisting body from the snow, ignoring the anxious bawling of the mother cow. His hands were too cold to tell whether the calf's body was warm enough to hold life.

"He's breathing!" shouted Dawn above the wind.

The flashlight in Dawn's hand was jerking too much for Logan to tell whether or not she was right. He didn't bother to argue. A single look over his shoulder told him what he had already guessed. There was so much snow blowing that the truck couldn't be seen even with headlights blazing.

"Mount up and ride for the barn!" he yelled.

As soon as he was in the saddle, Logan unbuttoned his coat and drew the calf against the warmth of his big body. The buckskin followed Bigfoot without hesitation. Logan let the reins go slack and held the edges of his coat around the calf as best he could. The wind's icy fingers clawed between the gaps in the sheepskin, chilling Logan despite the layers of clothes he wore underneath.

By the time the barn loomed out of the night, horses and riders were wearing a thick coating of wind-driven snow. Shorty was just pulling out in the pickup, sending its metal-studded tires churning through drifts that came and went with the wild wind. Logan cut off the truck, leaned down and yelled.

"Call the men in!"

The truck's airhorn sliced through the howl of the wind as Shorty drove along the road, calling the men in from the pasture. Dawn heard the sound and bit her lip against a cry of protest. She knew that it was futile to comb the pasture anymore. They simply couldn't see enough to justify the risk to the men.

Yet she hated to give up.

Logan rode right into the barn. The heat was like a blow. He dismounted in front of an empty stall. With one arm hugging the calf to his chest and the other half dragging

Dawn out of the saddle, Logan strode into the stall and dropped to his knees in the warm, fragrant straw. Dawn sat down and stripped off her snow-crusted ski mask, then took off her coat, spread it across her lap and held out her arms. He put the calf on the coat, curling the animal's cool, impossibly long legs beneath. He pulled off his own coat, covered the calf, and turned to take care of the horses.

Above the sound of the wind came the bawling of the cows. They had somehow sensed that their calves were inside the barn. The cows were huddled against the pasture fence as close as they could get to the warm stalls. Small sounds echoed through the barn as calves staggered to their feet, butting each other and the walls, bleating urgently, searching for milk.

Dawn leaned against the stall and felt carefully beneath Logan's jacket, seeking even the smallest sign of life. She repeated the search again and again, stroking the still body slowly, willing it to be alive.

Other calves are alive, she told herself wildly. *Why should this one die? Why can't I save this small, perfect life? Why do all the bright threads slip from my fingers, leaving only darkness and destruction?*

Gently Dawn smoothed the thick sheepskin jacket away from the calf's head. It took only a single look for her to know that she had been too late for this calf, too. She made no sound as her head tilted back against the stall. Eyes open, focused on nothing at all, she sat without moving except for her hand stroking the calf's cool russet hide.

"How's the—"

Logan's words died the instant he saw Dawn. Defeat was written in every line of her body. So was despair. She wasn't callous enough to ignore the small lives slipping uselessly into cold and death.

Gently he picked up the calf and set it aside. He wrapped Dawn's unresisting body in her jacket, pulled on his own coat and lifted Dawn into his arms. She stirred once, only to calm again at a murmured word. He took her to the

house, to his own bedroom. He undressed her and himself
pulled the covers over both of them and curled her along the
length of his body. Her unnatural stillness and silence cut
deeply into him. The need to comfort her was so great that
his hands trembled as he pulled her close.

"It's all right, little leaf," he murmured, stroking her
soothingly, rocking her against his body, wishing he could
take the despair from her into himself. "It will be better in
the morning."

"Will it?" she asked, her voice ragged. "Oh, God, it's so
dark!" Her hands moved over Logan's chest as though savoring the feel of something warm, something living. She
felt the sudden stirring of him against her thighs and knew
that tonight she would die if he didn't move within her
again. "Logan—" she said brokenly. "Logan, please. Hate
me in the morning if you must but please love me now!"

Logan's breath caught in his throat at the pleading in
Dawn's voice. When she said his name again he could bear
it no longer. He took her mouth, stilling her cries. She responded almost wildly, needing his touch so deeply that she
forgot the desolate pattern of their past. She held nothing of
herself back, for her need was greater than her fear. Her
hands moved down his body with a boldness and hunger
that she had never shown with him before. When she found
the hard thrust of his response, she made a deep sound of
satisfaction. Slowly, hotly, she explored him, glorying in the
life pulsing beneath her touch. Her hips moved even as her
hands did, sliding over him, telling him of her waiting softness.

He answered in a single powerful surge, giving himself to
her, filling her. She accepted him without reservation,
clinging to him, revealing her need and the wild trembling
deep inside her. Her response swept over him, taking away
his control, leaving only the driving rhythms of need, and
their bodies locked together in a primal release that left both
of them shaken.

Dawn fell asleep still joined to Logan, whispering his name and her love for him, not caring that nothing answered her but the heat of his skin next to hers.

Morning came in a flashing cataract of sunlight. The only evidence of yesterday's storm was in the sculpted mounds of snow rapidly melting beneath a warm wind. Spring had returned to the mountains, coming back redoubled as though to apologize for the winter storm. It wasn't the radiance or the warmth that woke Dawn; it was the insistent bawling of cattle. She stirred carefully, not wanting to wake Logan. She remembered her whispers of love the night before and felt fear turn darkly within her. She dreaded the moment he would wake up and the pattern would weave itself all over again, rejection and revenge.

Maybe it won't happen this time. Maybe—

The sound of an insistent knocking at the back door interrupted Dawn's thoughts. Logan didn't stir. Even asleep he looked exhausted. The thought of what riding in that blizzard must have done to his reserves of strength made Dawn bite her lip against a helpless protest. The knocking came with increased force. Without stopping to think, Dawn slid out of bed and pulled on the clothes Logan had taken off her the night before. She didn't notice him awaken silently as she shut the bedroom door behind her. She ran quickly down the stairs.

Shorty was at the back porch. "Logan up?" he asked gruffly.

"Not yet."

Shorty shifted his feet uncertainly. "Well, shoot. The cows is bawlin' and the calves is bawlin', and someone's gotta decide if it's time to turn 'em loose and sort themselves out. Then there's the fence. It's down at the south end. Lotta cows back up in them icy little draws, too. Should we leave 'em or should we bring 'em in?"

With growing impatience Dawn listened to the endless list of decisions to be made. All of them were routine. She had made the same kinds of decisions every day until the mo-

ment that Logan had won the Lazy W in a poker game. Now
he was upstairs, and exhaustion was written all over his
body. Every bit of her rebelled at the thought of waking him
so that he could restate the obvious to Shorty.

Briskly Dawn began telling Shorty what should be done
in what order and by whom. Shorty listened without asking
any questions, touched his hat in silent salute and left. She
closed the door, turned around—and saw Logan watching
her, his eyes all but black with anger.

"You almost got away with it," he grated between his
teeth. "You almost took Joe's revenge and turned it upside
down, just like your mama said she would. You and your
mama and the Lazy W. You never give up, do you."

"I just wanted you to sleep!" said Dawn desperately.

"Yeah. I'll bet. Well, I'm wide awake now." Logan
walked slowly toward her, his face drawn by rage into harsh
planes and angles. "You're really good, you know that? I
was feeling so sorry for you last night I damn near cried.
And then you begged for me and told me you loved me." He
made a disgusted sound. "Like hell. You're just like your
mama, selling yourself for a half share of the Lazy W." Logan's lips shaped a travesty of a smile. "Guess I'm a little
smarter than your daddy was. I got use of the body for
free."

Logan's eyes narrowed in contempt. "Pack up and get
out. When I come back I don't want to see any sign of you."

The porch door slammed behind Logan as he went out
into the pouring sunlight. For a terrible moment Dawn
could do no more than stand and stare through the window
at the man whose long-legged strides radiated rage. Last
night she had given herself to Logan the same way life gave
itself to the uncertain spring, hoping for the richness of
summer to come. But there would be no summer for her this
year. Like the calves she had found too late, she had simply
lost life's gamble.

I don't want to see any sign of you.

Methodically Dawn went into the living room and began to stir up the fire in the hearth. When the flames leaped high, she went through the house and took every curtain, every scarf, every scrap of color she had woven into the bleak pattern of Logan's life. They went from her hand into the fire and she watched them burn to ash.

Then she looked up from the hearth to the old Bowie knife Logan kept on the mantel.

Beyond the house the bawling of cattle nearly drowned out the shouts of men trying to urge calves from the barn into the pasture to be claimed by their frantic mothers. Logan watched the calves being licked thoroughly from neck to tail while they butted their mothers and drank warm, rich milk. Looking at the sun and the calves and the blush of green showing across the windswept pasture, it was hard to believe that the nightmare of ice and snow and dying calves had ever happened.

Then the view was replaced by an image from the long night—despairing eyes the color of spring, a face as pale as snow and slender fingers stroking a dead calf.

With a muttered curse Logan turned and stalked toward the barn. Turk and another cowhand rode out as Logan arrived. They were on their way to sweep the pasture for calves that might need help. Orders that Dawn, not Logan, had given. Orders that she had no right to give.

The Lazy W is Garrett property. Joe's revenge. And it will stay that way. Mary Sue won't have the last word, the last drop of Garrett blood.

Logan walked down the rows of barn stalls. Bigfoot and the buckskin were still inside, resting three-legged after their grueling night. Logan stopped at the next stall. It was where he had found Dawn. The image came to him again with horrible clarity. Seeing her stroking that dead calf had turned him inside out. Her eyes had been—empty.

Like this morning when he had told her to get off the ranch. Empty. Like the way the house would be after she left. Empty. Like revenge. Empty.

Like him.

Logan's long fingers gripped the top of the stall until they ached. Memories poured over him, a tangle of Joe's laments about Mary Sue from the deep past and Logan's own recent memories of Dawn giving herself to him and never counting the cost. And it had cost her. He was as sure of that as he was of the emptiness in her eyes, in himself. He had taken everything from Dawn and given her nothing in return.

Like Mary Sue with Joe.

"No," whispered Logan.

Horror crawled over him as he realized that he had become the very thing he loathed, a person who could take love and twist it to his own cold purposes. Dawn's love.

I loved you.

The echo from three years ago blended with the image of Dawn's despair and the more recent echoes of her husky voice murmuring love against his mouth in the instants before she fell asleep in his arms. The thought of never hearing her say those words again went through him like an icy wind. He wanted to know those gentle moments with Dawn again. He had to. It was a need so deep, so absolute, that it could not be denied or ignored.

I'm not like Joe! Logan cried to the silent barn. *I'm not that weak!*

No, came the soundless answer. *You're like Mary Sue. Screw or be screwed. You made your choice and you won. What the hell are you whining about?*

But this didn't feel like winning. It felt like being caught in the endless, tearing instant of losing. It felt like seeing forever the dead calf curled in Dawn's lap and knowing that she was breaking inside and there was nothing he could do to make time run backward, to hold back the icy storm and the useless deaths, to turn the world inside out and make it right for the woman he loved.

Because he did love Dawn.

He had loved her for years with an intensity that terrified him, so he had struck out at her, driving her away. She had known the risks of caring for him and had found the courage to grow anyway, to reach for the uncertain spring of love despite the bitter reality of winter. He had only clung to winter's cruel certainties, afraid to reach for fire and life. She had poured out her warmth heedlessly, recklessly, giving herself to the man she loved. He had given her—

Emptiness.

And then he had sent her away.

Logan turned and ran back to the ranch house. He raced through the cold kitchen and the colorless living room, feeling a new kind of fear sink into him. Not a fear of the past, but of the future. Emptiness and an icy wind.

Only a few bright threads of Dawn's weaving remained on the hearth, but they were enough to tell Logan how much beauty had been burned to ash at his cruel command: *I don't want to see any sign of you when I get back.* Then he remembered the tapesty upstairs, light growing out of darkness, fire burning out of the depths of night.

And his question: *What do you do when a pattern doesn't work?*

And her answer: *I cut it from the loom and burn it to ash.*

Logan wanted to cry out but he had no voice, only the razor wind of loss blowing through his soul, chilling him. He spun around and took the stairs three at a time, praying that he hadn't reached for warmth too late.

Dawn stood motionless in front of her grandmother's loom with Logan's heavy knife in her hand. She didn't hear him stop at the doorway and then cross the room quickly behind her. She didn't hear anything but the past wailing around her like a blizzard. And each razor crystal of ice cutting her was a separate lost hope, a distinct memory. And the wind itself was the unspeakably bitter knowledge that she had done nothing for the man she loved but to make him more cruel, more cold, driving him even farther from life's warmth.

With hands that shook, Dawn lifted the knife over the failed pattern of her love.

"No!" Logan's hand shot out as he took the knife from her and sent it spinning across the room.

Dawn simply looked at the hard fingers wrapped around her wrist, unable to believe that he was there, that he had stopped her. He turned her unresisting body toward him and tilted her face up to his. Her eyes were wide, empty. He felt her shiver uncontrollably and realized that her skin was cold to his touch. Swiftly he unbuttoned his heavy sheepskin coat and pulled her inside, wrapping her in warmth, holding her, rocking her against his body as his lips brushed gently over her face.

"Stay with me," he said urgently. "I don't care anymore about revenge or Joe or the Lazy W. I'll give you the ranch if that's what you want. It's yours. Everything I have is yours. Just don't leave me. Don't. Leave. I—"

Logan's voice broke as he buried his face in Dawn's unbound hair. She tried to move her head, tried to see or touch his face, but he held her so tightly that she couldn't move.

"I don't want—" cried Dawn.

"Don't say no," he whispered raggedly. "You can't say no."

His mouth found hers, brushed warmth over her lips, cherished her softness, silently begged for just a bit of the warmth she had once given to him so recklessly, so generously.

With a small cry she yielded to him, needing him. She felt the tremor that shook his powerful body as she softened against him. She had felt him tremble before, but only in passion. This wasn't passion. It was something deeper, something stronger than lust and the lessons of the past, stronger than hatred and revenge, stronger even than winter's cruel winds. This was as wild as spring, as hot and wrenching as the tears she tasted on his lips.

"I never wanted the ranch," she said, her voice husky with emotion. "It was you, Logan, always you. I loved you before I even knew I could love."

His trembling hands framed her face. "Yes," he said, kissing her swiftly, gently, a kiss for each heartbeat bringing life to him, to her. "It was like that for me. I want you to be my wife, my woman, the mother of my children. Most of all I want you, just you," he whispered, holding her. "I need you so much it scares the hell out of me. I love you, Dawn. I love you more than anything on earth."

Dawn looked at Logan's taut face for an instant, afraid to believe what she had heard. With a soft, wild cry she stood on tiptoe as she reached for him, wanting only to be close to him. Even as she strained against him, he lifted her, surrounding her, giving her words of love, weaving the two of them together as deeply as the flame figures she had woven for him.

And like the tapestry lovers safe within the loom's embrace, Logan and Dawn would live forever within the fire of spring.

 Silhouette Desire

COMING NEXT MONTH

EYE OF THE TIGER—Diana Palmer
Eleanor had once loved Keegan—handsome, wealthy and to the
manor born. The differences between them were great, and time
hadn't changed them. But the passion was still there too.

DECEPTIONS—Annette Broadrick
Although Lisa and Drew were separated, the movie stars agreed
to make a film together. Would on-camera sparks rekindle
passionate flames off-camera as well?

HOT PROPERTIES—Suzanne Forster
Sunny and Gray were rival talk-show hosts, brought together in a
ratings ploy. Their on-air chemistry sent the numbers soaring—
but not as high as Sunny's heart!

LAST YEAR'S HUNK—Marie Nicole
Travis wanted to be known for his acting, not his biceps.
C. J. Parker could help him, but business and pleasure don't
always mix . . . and she had more than business in mind.

PENNIES IN THE FOUNTAIN—Robin Elliott
Why was Megan James involved with big-time crook
Frankie Bodeen? Detective Steel Danner had to know. He'd fallen
in love at first sight, and he was determined to prove
her innocence.

CHALLENGE THE FATES—Jo Ann Algermissen
Her child might be alive! Had Autumn and Luke been victims of
a cruel lie—and could they pick up the pieces and right the
wrongs of the past?

AVAILABLE THIS MONTH:

THE FIRE OF SPRING
Elizabeth Lowell

THE SANDCASTLE MAN
Nicole Monet

LOGICAL CHOICE
Amanda Lee

CONFESS TO APOLLO
Suzanne Carey

SPLIT IMAGES
Naomi Horton

UNFINISHED RHAPSODY
Gina Caimi

Take 4 Silhouette Intimate Moments novels FREE

Then preview 4 brand new Silhouette Intimate Moments® novels —delivered to your door every month—for 15 days as soon as they are published. When you decide to keep them, you pay just $2.25 each ($2.50 each, in Canada), *with no shipping, handling, or other charges of any kind!*

Silhouette Intimate Moments novels are not for everyone. They were created to give you a more detailed, more exciting reading experience, filled with romantic fantasy, intense sensuality, and stirring passion.

The first 4 Silhouette Intimate Moments novels are absolutely FREE and without obligation, yours to keep. You can cancel at any time.

You'll also receive a FREE subscription to the Silhouette Books Newsletter as long as you remain a member. Each issue is filled with news on upcoming titles, interviews with your favorite authors, even their favorite recipes.

To get your 4 FREE books, fill out and mail the coupon today!

Silhouette Books, 120 Brighton Rd., P.O. Box 5084, Clifton, NJ 07015-5084

Clip and mail to: Silhouette Books,
120 Brighton Road, P.O. Box 5084, Clifton, NJ 07015-5084*

YES. Please send me 4 FREE Silhouette Intimate Moments novels. Unless you hear from me after I receive them, send me 4 brand new Silhouette Intimate Moments novels to preview each month. I understand you will bill me just $2.25 each, a total of $9.00 (in Canada, $2.50 each, a total of $10.00)—with no shipping, handling, or other charges of any kind. There is no minimum number of books that I must buy, and I can cancel at any time. The first 4 books are mine to keep. *Silhouette Intimate Moments available in Canada through subscription only.*

IM-SUB-1   **BM1826**

Name _____ (please print) _____

Address _____ Apt. # _____

City _____ State/Prov. _____ Zip/Postal Code _____

* In Canada, mail to: Silhouette Canadian Book Club,
320 Steelcase Rd. E., Markham, Ontario, L3R 2M1, Canada
Terms and prices subject to change.
SILHOUETTE INTIMATE MOMENTS is a service mark and registered trademark.

The Silhouette Cameo Tote Bag Now available for just $6.99

Handsomely designed in blue and bright pink, its stylish good looks make the Cameo Tote Bag an attractive accessory. The Cameo Tote Bag is big and roomy (13″ square), with reinforced handles and a snap-shut top. You can buy the Cameo Tote Bag for $6.99, plus $1.50 for postage and handling.

Send your name and address with check or money order for $6.99 (plus $1.50 postage and handling), a total of $8.49 to:

Silhouette Books
120 Brighton Road
P.O. Box 5084
Clifton, NJ 07015-5084
ATTN: Tote Bag

SIL-T-1

The Silhouette Cameo Tote Bag can be purchased pre-paid only. No charges will be accepted. **Please** allow 4 to 6 weeks for delivery.

Arizona and **N.Y. State** Residents Please Add Sales Tax

Offer not available in Canada.